S0-AAC-894

# The Island Keeper

## by Harry Mazer

DELACORTE PRESS/NEW YORK

Published by
DELACORTE PRESS
1 Dag Hammarskjold Plaza
New York, N.Y. 10017

Manufactured in the United States of America

First printing

LIBRARY OF CONGRESS CATALOGING IN PUBLICATION DATA

Mazer, Harry.
    The island keeper.

    SUMMARY: Longing to disappear after the death
of her beloved younger sister, 16-year-old Cleo
runs away from her overprotective and oppressive
family and goes to a remote island where she is the
only human inhabitant.
    [1. Runaways—Fiction.   2. Survival—Fiction.
3. Islands—Fiction.   4. Family life—Fiction]
I. Title.
PZ7.M47397Is    [Fic]      80-68735
ISBN 0-440-03976-2

*To the young who stand at the
threshold of an uncertain world. Courage.*

# THE ISLAND KEEPER

# Chapter 1

Cleo Murphy was late boarding the flight from Chicago to New York because Eric Weeser, her father's secretary, insisted on coming in with her and carrying her bags to the American Airlines booth even though she could handle her two suitcases better than he could. And then he stood there telling her how "time heals all wounds," even those of the "recent tragic events." That was the way he talked. He was an old man, and he droned on as if he had all the time in the world.

Cleo almost didn't make her flight and had to squeeze past the man on the aisle seat. She had poured her grandmother's perfume all over herself, and hated the way she smelled. And from the way the man next to her was leaning into the aisle he hated it, too.

She tried to pretend to herself she wasn't fat and that even if she was it didn't matter. But traveling in an airplane, squeezed into those little seats, there was no way to hide her size. First class had more room—the family could afford it, too—but her father wouldn't let any of them travel first class as a matter of principle. Her father had lots of principles. Don't flaunt your wealth. Don't show off. Don't act better than anyone else. Of course the Murphys *knew* they were better. Richer, more talented, better bred—better taste. Just *better.* But they had to pretend they were like everyone else.

As the plane taxied toward takeoff, Cleo sat back, closing her eyes. The sound of the rising engines, the roar of the takeoff, drowned every other sound. She gripped the arms of her seat. She'd flown all her life, but she never got used to takeoffs and didn't relax till they were high in the air, the sound of the engines muffled, monotonous, and steady.

So many flights through the years. Back and forth to school several times every year, and then the summer camps, and sometimes going to Dundee. Waiting in airports to be picked up . . . waiting for her sister to come from her school . . . looking forward to the good times when Jam and she would be together again. . . . They weren't together that much, maybe two weeks over Easter, and two more at Christmas, and then those few weeks between the end of school and the beginning of camp.

Cleo had been sent away to school when she was eight. Jam, who was four years younger, stayed home till she was seven, then she, too, was sent away. Different schools, different camps. Her grandmother chose them all, but after a while she always found something wrong. In eight years—she was sixteen now—Cleo had attended four different schools. It became harder and harder to make friends. She was forever packing and unpacking, coming or going, or getting ready to go. Sometimes she felt like a package her grandmother kept wrapping and rewrapping and sending off to this place or that.

And Jam, her sister, would be alive now if they had been allowed to stay together. Cleo felt sure of that. She leaned forward, pressed her head against the seat in front of her. Stop thinking about Jam. What good was it?

"You feeling all right?" the man sitting next to her asked. He had on a gold watch and gold cufflinks.

Cleo nodded. All that gold reminded her of her father. Was the man an agent of her father's, sent to keep an eye on his crazy daughter? Her father wore a gold ring on each hand, a gold wrist band, and gold cufflinks. Her grandmother loved to help her son with the cufflinks, laying out his clothes, too—the designer shirts and matching ties.

Her grandmother despised the jeans and plaid shirts Cleo felt comfortable in. Today Cleo was dressed like a lady—batiste blouse, white linen skirt, pantie hose, girdle, Greek sandals—all things her grandmother had bought for her. To her grandmother the essence of being female was to wear skirts, be pleasant, not to disagree, and never to have loud opinions or offensive manners or odors.

Only this morning her grandmother had said, "You can be so attractive if you try." Attractive for what? She felt grotesque in these clothes. She would never be the lady her grandmother wanted her to be. She was the opposite of her grand-mother in every way. She was female, like her, but that was it. Even to be thinking about clothes now was sickening. She hated the way her mind had slid away from what mattered. Jam, the only person she loved in the world, was dead. Cleo wanted to remember, wanted that pain. She didn't want to forget. *Jessica . . . Jessie . . . Jam . . . my Jam. I want to see you. . . . I won't cry. . . . Just let me see you once more. . . .*

No, she couldn't keep thinking about it. There

were things to do. On a folded sheet of paper she had written out her escape plan. *Eight Steps to Freedom.* Step one was this flight from Chicago to New York. They were under way. The plane had gotten safely into the air. Everything was going smoothly. Ridiculous, really, this making of escape plans, like a Nancy Drew mystery. But it was reassuring.

Step one was easy. It would end when they landed at Kennedy Airport. Step two was a lot harder. Call White Mountain Camp and in her grandmother's voice tell them that Cleo was not returning to camp this summer. Cleo sighed and let her eyes run over the other six steps. One step at a time. Don't get discouraged. Today, in just a few hours, she was going to disappear completely.

*Disappear completely.* She could almost taste the words, they suited her so exactly.

Her mother had died nine years ago in a senseless accident when her car had hit a runaway horse. And now her sister in another stupid freak accident. How could they both be dead? How could it be? The two people she loved most in the world. Was it fair? It was so unfair. Why wasn't pain divided equally in the world? If people had to die, let there be an equal distribution! Why just her? But then she thought of the wealth her family had that other families didn't have: the money and houses, the people who served them. There was nothing equal in the world. Not money, not pain. Nothing was ever given or taken away equally, or fairly, or justly.

She looked out the window. The engines seemed unnaturally loud and rough. Were they going to fail? First her mother, then Jam, now it would be her. She imagined the plane falling. The long silence, then the drop . . . and screams. . . . She saw herself in the aisle, reaching out for a child, any child. She'd pull her down under the seats. She'd protect her, cover her with her body. She'd save her, yes . . . the way she had not been able to save Jam.

# Chapter 2

Her grandmother could never understand what Jam and Cleo had to talk about all the time. "What are you girls talking about now?"

"Nothing, Grandma." Jam and Cleo never talked in front of her. Nor did they talk to anyone else the way they talked to each other. They were different together than they were with other people. With everyone else Jam was wild. She never wanted to sleep, would go dancing down the halls at night, peek down the stairs at their father's company, and make so much noise the women would notice her and call her down and fuss over her. She was nervy, irrepressible, fresh—said things Cleo never dared say. Cleo was the brooder, the "sullen one," who looked and watched but kept what she felt locked inside. She was herself only with Jam, and Jam was the same with Cleo. That was their secret, the thing they never shared with anyone else. That was why nobody could ever come between them.

Years ago, at night, when Jam had trouble sleeping she'd lie with her head on Cleo's shoulder and close her eyes. "Cleo, tell me about mother." It was a secret that they talked about their mother. Mustn't talk about her in front of Grandmother. That was morbid.

"Jam, when I think of Mother, I think of someone tall and pretty, like you." Cleo would always start the story the same way. "Her hair was thick like yours, too, and she wore it in two pigtails the way you do."

"Really, Cleo? Even though she was grown-up?"

"Yes. That was the sort of person she was. She was young and pretty when she married Daddy. He was older and famous."

"And very rich."

"Yes. He loved Mother and she loved him."

"And then what happened?"

"Then they had two pretty girl babies. First Cleo and then Jessica." The story was always the same. It was better that way.

"And they were happy? Mother loved us, didn't she?"

"Oh, yes."

"She was really nice?"

"Yes, yes." Jam knew all the answers. She'd heard the story a hundred times. But that didn't matter. What counted was talking about mother.

"The nicest mother in the world. She loved to cuddle us. She was soft and warm, that's what I remember. So warm, Jam."

"Cleo, if Mother had lived . . . everything would have been different."

"Yes."

"Tell me what happened. Tell me, Cleo."

"They had a fight one day . . . she and Daddy. A bad fight."

"Why did they fight?"

"I don't know. I was so small. He was away a lot. Grandmother ran the house. Mother didn't have anything to do."

"She had us."

"Yes, but she couldn't do anything else. The cook cooked, and Mrs. Terrero took care of the house, and Anna watched us, and Grandmother watched everybody."

"Did they have a lot of fights?"

"A lot of fights. I used to hear them and cry in my bed. So that day Mother took us in the car. She was running away with us. You were three years old, and I was seven. You sat between Mother and me."

"And then, Cleo?"

"You remember, Jam."

"No, I want you to tell me."

"What I remember, Jam, is the horse. His head came through the windshield. It was a runaway. I don't remember being thrown from the car. It was winter. It was snowing. A lot of snow. Mother was sitting on the ground. Blood was coming out of her mouth. She was moving her hands, trying to speak, and someone was screaming."

"That was me."

"Yes. You were screaming. That's all I remember."

"I remember when they sent you away to school, Cleo."

"I do, too."

As Cleo got older, she hated coming home. Her grandmother didn't like her, and she didn't know what to think of her father, he was so distant. She had hoped that when she got older he'd be more interested in her, but it hadn't happened yet.

Everything was stiff and artificial when the girls were home, and the four of them had their meals together. Jam and Cleo were expected to dress, make conversation, and show what they had learned in their schools. Afterward, back at school, for weeks after every vacation Cleo had bad dreams about those formal meals. She still remembered that breakfast at the beginning of the summer, the last time she saw Jam. Cleo was leaving that afternoon for White Mountain Riding Camp in New Hampshire, and Jam would be going off later that week to a sailing camp on Lake Michigan.

Their grandmother, upright in a jade-green dress buttoned to her chin, presided at the table. Her still-thick blond hair was pulled back from her face, her eyes were made up so they shone like black lacquer. "I hope you're going to make an effort to take some weight off this summer, Cleo." She was at Cleo's father's right, pouring his coffee from the silver service.

Cleo smiled—nodded her head slightly—didn't reply. Always, she said as little as she dared.

"Cleo doesn't have to diet," Jam said. "She's perfect the way she is."

"Oh?" their grandmother said.

And their handsome father, at the head of the table, remote, golden, like a prince, smoothed a crumb from his vest and turned a page of *The Wall Street Journal*. This was old, boring stuff to him.

"You must learn to eat less, Cleo." Her grandmother pointed to her own breakfast: a single egg in a porcelain cup, a slice of unbuttered toast, a small bowl of yellow grapes. "I haven't gained or lost an ounce in forty years. You'll bear me out, Robert?"

"I bear you out, Mother." He didn't lift his head from the paper.

"Are you going to make a concentrated effort to lose weight this summer? Mitzi Stoner promised me that she was going to keep a careful eye on you. You'd do well to follow her advice."

Cleo sat there, a strained smile on her face, lining up the silver along the edge of the cloth. The odor of her grandmother's powder, a scent like wilted roses, sickened her.

"What did they teach you at St. Ives? You don't speak. I'm beginning to dislike that school."

"It's all right," Cleo said, driven to talk. She dreaded the thought that she would be put into another school. "I like it there."

"Like—what does that matter? The question is, Do they educate? St. Ives certainly hasn't given you the foggiest preparation for table conversation. You don't talk, Cleo, you don't eat, and yet you blow up like a balloon. Here. Do something useful." She pushed her egg cup across to Cleo and watched as she cracked the egg.

There was a trick to it. You had to tap it carefully around the end, and then the shell could be lifted from the top like a cap. Cleo hit the shell too hard, too low, smashed the whole top. Yellow oozed over her fingers and onto the tablecloth.

"It's a shame your father has to see this." Her grandmother rang for Mrs. Terrero. "Your fingers really are as fat and inept as the rest of you. Here, wipe your hands."

"Grandmother!" Jam jumped up. "It wasn't Cleo's fault."

"You're not to interrupt, young lady. Please sit down!"

They sat in silence while Mrs. Terrero brought their grandmother a fresh egg, then cracked the top perfectly.

Later Jam came up to Cleo's room while she finished packing. Her suitcases were open on the bed. "I suppose you want me to help you, fat fingers," Jam said.

"Yes, I do, fat mouth."

Jam shook her finger at Cleo. "I don't know what they teach you at St. Ives."

"Sit down like a lady, please, and shut up. I want to talk to you."

Jam sank to the floor and folded her hands in her lap, head cocked, lips primly closed. A perfect imitation of the good, attentive little girl.

"Listen, are you going to write to me this summer or not?"

"I always write to you, Cleo."

"Not those stingy postcards. That's not writing. I want a letter from you. When I write you, write back. And postcards don't count." She folded shirts into the suitcase.

"Are you going to have a boyfriend this summer?" Jam asked.

"How should I know? There's only Doug, Mitzi's son. And with fifty girls ogling him, he's not looking at me."

"Why not? You're worth looking at. You're as pretty as any of them. Prettier."

Cleo grabbed her sister, hugged and kissed her, only Jam turned at the last moment, and the kiss Cleo had aimed for her cheek almost caught her in the eye.

"If that's the best you can kiss, no wonder you don't have a boyfriend. Here, let me do that." Jam reached for the suitcase and carried it to the door. "How do you like them muscles? Getting bigger every day." She stuck out her chest. "And that ain't all. You think the boys are going to notice me this summer?"

"You just watch yourself," Cleo said. "Don't do anything stupid."

Jam gave her a big grin. "Like what?"

"You know what I'm talking about." It was hard for Cleo to talk about boys and sex because she'd never had a boyfriend. "This isn't sour grapes, Jam. You'll probably have a boyfriend before me —but don't rush. I know you. Don't throw yourself at the first boy who looks at you. You've got time. You're not even thirteen yet."

"Three weeks away. I thought I'd have a boyfriend by now! Thirteen and never been kissed." She picked up the bottle of perfume their grandmother had given Cleo and took a whiff. "Whew, nice. Sexy. Will you call me on my birthday?"

"Don't I always?"

"I'm going to miss you."

"I'll miss you, too."

"Do you think we'll ever be together?" Jam pushed aside the curtain and looked out the window. "Maybe next summer," she said dreamily, "they'll let us go to the island again."

Cleo shook her head. "You know Dad doesn't even like the lake anymore."

"I still dream about the island. Wouldn't it be gorgeous, Cleo?"

"No boys there."

"I wouldn't care. Just the two of us on the island . . ." She turned around and saw that Cleo had finished packing. "You're going now? Already?"

They said good-bye upstairs in Cleo's room. It was their special good-bye, just the two of them. "Remember to write," Cleo said. They hugged and kissed. The last time she saw Jam, Cleo was downstairs, waiting for the car to come around, and Jam was hanging out a window, yelling, "Don't kiss any bedbugs."

Only a week later the call came from her grandmother. Cleo took it in the barn, where she had been saddling up a horse for one of the younger girls. "Cleo? Something's happened. There's been an accident . . . a terrible accident."

"Jam?" she said. Behind her there was a terrible noise. One of the horses was kicking the stall.

Her grandmother was crying, choking broken cries. ". . . an accident . . . a terrible accident . . . the lake . . ."

Cleo held the phone away from her ear. Her grandmother's voice came from a distance, but she heard each word distinctly. Jam had been out on the lake alone. The water was choppy. "They're not supposed to be in the boats alone. Nobody knows what happened. Maybe the boom hit her head. When they righted the boat, she was tangled in the ropes. You'll come home at once."

"Yes," Cleo said. "I'll come today."

"Well . . . are you all right?" her grandmother said. She asked that several times.

"Yes, yes," Cleo said. She didn't cry. Her grandmother expected her to cry, but Cleo couldn't. She felt blocked off. There were no openings in her, no cracks, no way for tears to get out.

At the funeral a long line of black cars curved down to the gate, and still more were coming. The sun shone. A hot wind blew. The fringed awning over the grave snapped in the wind. Her father was hatless, his golden hair stirred by the wind. Her grandmother, all in black, her face hidden by a veil, seemed smaller than Cleo remembered. Everything was wrong, out of proportion, like a picture with all the wrong things in it.

The minister talked about her sister, extolling her. "This young woman . . . in the prime of life . . ." He was paid to be there, to say those words . . . and all the people with their sober faces and black clothes, here because of her father. They wouldn't dare not appear. None of them had come for Jam.

Velvet ropes waited to lower the golden casket into a carpeted hole. Cleo stepped forward. The sun off the casket blinded her. *Jam . . . my sister . . .* She tried to speak. "No. . . . No . . ." she cried. Her father's secretary, Eric Weeser, caught her, held her tight. "My dear," he whispered, "control yourself. . . ."

Yes, yes. She understood. People were watching. People . . . yes, people were watching. She was Cleo Murphy. Murphys didn't break down. Nothing could be changed by emotional displays.

Emptiness swept through her. She felt hollowed out. She waited for the wind to carry her away like a straw. She stared at her father, her grandmother. Who were they? She didn't recognize them anymore. Jam was dead. The one person in the world she loved . . . who loved her. . . . *Jam was dead.* She was alone . . . alone . . . alone. . . . So many times she'd thought of leaving, and hadn't because of Jam. Nothing held her now. Nothing. No one. There was no reason to stay.

# Chapter 3

For Cleo, eating didn't have anything to do with hunger. It was the way she reacted, almost automatically, to tension. Food was what she turned to whenever she was nervous or scared. When the plane landed at Kennedy Airport the first thing she did was find a lunch counter and order a chocolate shake, fries, and a plain burger.

She wolfed down the burger and ordered another. A man passed behind her. Her head jerked up. Was she being followed?

No, her father and grandmother weren't even thinking about her. As far as they were concerned she was well on her way to White Mountain Riding Camp. If everything went the way she'd planned, it would be weeks before they knew. Her father would have theories. He was big on theories and thinking things through to their logical conclusions. He'd think kidnapping first, because that was money and he was a rich man. But then, why hadn't her abductors gotten in touch with him? Foul play, then. Not a pleasant thought. He'd just gotten through burying one daughter. Damned nuisance, really. He'd want a body, though, before considering foul play seriously.

He'd have other theories. She might have run away. Not really a serious consideration. Cleo the blob do something on her own? Not likely. What would she run away for? She had been coddled, fed, taken care of, given everything money could buy. She certainly had enough brains to appreciate that!

Her grandmother would be more suspicious than her father, but neither of them would think of Duck Island. Even though her father owned it, he hadn't been there in years, and if he did think of it he'd never connect the island with Cleo. She'd only been there once, three years ago, and he didn't know what it had meant to her . . . that she remembered every moment of the two weeks she and Jam had spent there that one summer.

Frank Garrity, the caretaker at Dundee, was the only adult who'd come to the island during those two weeks, and he'd only come to check up on them. It was private, away from everything, so far out on Big Clear Lake that nobody ever came there. Cleo had been thirteen that summer, Jam nine. It had been the happiest time they'd ever had together.

She sucked up the last bit of shake, then ran the straw around the bottom of the container. Cleo, the human vacuum cleaner. Fat slob. Can't choose an island that's not your father's. Not original or brave enough to go someplace you don't know . . . a city . . . anywhere else . . .

She looked at her escape plan and checked off number one. She had arrived at Kennedy. Easy. Step two would be a lot harder. Call Mitzi Stoner at White Mountain Camp and pretend to be Mrs. Murphy, then tell Mitzi that Cleo wasn't returning to camp this summer.

She got several dollars worth of change at the cash register and chose a phone booth in one of the busiest corridors. Her knees were trembly. She sat there for a while, catching her breath. People rushed by. No one looked at her. Stacking and restacking the quarters and dimes . . . practicing what she'd say . . . *Mrs. Stoner*—Would her grandmother call her that, or Mitzi? No, her grandmother wouldn't be familiar. *Mrs. Stoner, this is Mrs. Murphy. Cleo's grandmother.*

She won't believe you, stupid. She'll know right away. Forget it. You still have time to catch the plane for camp.

That nasty spiteful voice, the no voice, the you-can't voice, the you're-too-slow voice, too fat, toooo stupid! Sometimes she could make it shut up. Sometimes it was so strong it was the only voice she heard. Now it was racketing in her ears.

You'll never get away with it, dumbo.

Shut up! She dialed.

"Operator," a man said. Cleo cleared her throat and gave the operator the office number at White Mountain Riding Camp, then deposited the money.

In moments, the director's familiar chatty voice over the phone sent a chill of weakness and doubt through Cleo. "Mitzi Stoner here." Cleo couldn't speak. "Hello? Mitzi Stoner here."

"This . . . this is Mrs. Murphy." She raised her voice, assuming her grandmother's firm, precise tones. "It's about Cleo—"

"How is she, Mrs. Murphy? And how are *you*? I've been thinking about that poor girl—losing her sister. I haven't been able to sleep. How is she taking it? It's an awful burden for a young person."

"She's handling it well, under the circumstances."

"I know it. Oh, that girl. We sure love her dearly. Helen and I were just talking, wondering when Cleo'd be back with us. You've got a terrific gal in that granddaughter of yours."

Cleo could see Mitzi sprawled out in her folding canvas chair in front of the office, wearing wrinkled shorts, white socks, and clumpy Buster Brown shoes. She said the same thing to every parent. "Terrific gal, that daughter of yours. We sure love her dearly!"

"Mrs. Stoner"—Cleo couldn't let her ramble on—"I'm terribly sorry, but Cleo won't be returning to camp this year. She's not—well." Cleo's voice broke.

"Oh, I understand! Please don't say another word, Mrs. Murphy. We all know about your terrible, terrible loss. If there's anything we can do . . . we'll take care of everything on our end, Mrs. Murphy. Pack up Cleo's things and send them along—"

"No!" Cleo had a vision of her trunk arriving home without her. That was something she hadn't thought of. "Mrs. Stoner, you'll have to hold everything." Her grandmother couldn't have said it more commandingly. "We'll be traveling this summer. Cleo needs a change of scene. The house in Chicago will be closed."

"No trouble at all," Mitzi said heartily. "Whatever you think best, Mrs. Murphy. Ahh, Mrs. Murphy—the charges. Cleo was going to be with us all summer. I wonder if you would want us to make an adjustment . . . a refund?"

"That won't be necessary. Just leave things as they are."

"Fine. Thank you, Mrs. Murphy."

Cleo hung up and just sat for a moment taking deep breaths. She felt limp. After a while she joined the crowds and collected her suitcases. They were the only ones still going around on the carrousel.

Step three of her escape plan. Go to the nearest ladies' room. The booths were all taken. A woman waited, smoothing her hair in front of the mirror. Cleo caught a glimpse of herself—a fat, gross girl with sweat patches under her arms, wrinkled blouse, face shiny with sweat and excitement.

The moment a booth was free she slipped inside. One suitcase caught in the door. She yanked it in, locked the door. Her face was boiling. She kicked off her sandals, the batiste blouse, the white linen skirt, the pantie girdle she hated. She felt she was throwing off a hateful identity. Never again would she wear anything she didn't want to. She changed quickly. Was anyone watching? Where? Under the partition? Why? Who cared what a fat, crazy girl was doing?

She stuffed the clothes into one of the suitcases and put on a white T-shirt and blue denim overalls. She took jeans, shorts, underwear, socks, some T-shirts and sweaters, and stuffed them all into the orange knapsack she'd packed into the suitcase. Emptied her wallet and tossed it into the suitcase, too, put money and ID into the bib pocket of the overalls, tore up everything else—cards and photos—and flushed them down the toilet.

She emerged from the booth, knapsack on her back, dragging the suitcases. She was terribly excited. Up to this moment it had just been talk, something she told herself she would do but wasn't sure she'd have the nerve for. What had she ever done on her own? Nothing.

In a corner by a wall of lockers she emptied the contents of the suitcases into a plastic bag. The luggage went into the locker. She pocketed the key and carried the plastic bag with her as she left the building. In every trash can she passed she left something else. The wallet in one, her skirt in another, sandals in a third . . .

She boarded a bus for New York City. In front of the East Side Terminal, she dropped the locker key down a sewer, then took a cab to the Port Authority and found out when the next bus left for Toronto.

Step number five of her escape plan. She was disappearing. Nobody in these crowds would remember a fat girl in overalls and a white T-shirt.

# Chapter 4

"Hi, I'm Glenn. Can I help you, miss?" The clerk in the outdoor store in Toronto was short with soft, appealing eyes. "What can we do for you this afternoon?"

Cleo looked around. She was still bleary from the all-night bus ride from New York. There were so many things on shelves, hanging on the walls, and dangling from the ceiling . . . jackets, boots, knives, rolled-up tents and metal poles, all kinds of knapsacks and bags. She pointed to a large blue knapsack with a metal frame. "That . . . and a sleeping bag, please."

"Down?" he said.

"What?"

"Down-filled?"

"Oh, uh, sure."

"Will it be cold where you're going?"

"I don't know."

"Well, where are you going?"

She panicked. *Where?* "Uh, Big Clear—" How stupid! "My, uh, boyfriend and I are going on a canoe trip," she said. "I guess it might get cold at night." Her face was hot. He must be suspicious. No, *amused.* Laughing his head off. *Her* have a boyfriend? That fat cow?

"I want your very best sleeping bag," she said, putting on her superior Murphy voice.

He brought her a rolled-up sleeping bag that he set beside the knapsack. "Top of the line," he said, patting it. "This will keep you warm at forty below. What else will you be needing, miss?"

She really felt at a loss . . . knew so little about camping! The times she'd gone hiking, the overnights she'd been on at various camps, even the time she and Jam had gone to the island, everything had been taken care of. What did she have to know? Frank had taken her and Jam to Duck Island in one of the motorboats. The cabin had been ready for them. He'd brought them food and firewood, even ice cream on the days he came to check up on them. At her summer camps, she hiked with the other girls, and when they arrived the camp truck was waiting with sleeping bags, tents all set up, and steaks on the fire. Sixteen years old and she'd never done anything for herself. What had her education been worth? What did she know about life? How to stand up when an adult entered the room, and how to say "I beg your pardon" in horrible French.

"What else do I need?" she asked. "Uh, my boyfriend gave me a list, but I lost it."

The salesman, Glenn, was sympathetic. "To begin with, I'd have a ground cloth so your sleeping bag won't get wet. It's also a poncho." Cleo nodded. "A foam pad to soften the ground."

"No." She rejected that. She had enough padding of her own. Besides, there were cots in the cabin, maybe even mattresses.

He sold her a mess kit with a frying pan–nesting pot combination, a ring with utensils, a folding bucket. "A flashlight, remember, with some extra batteries," he said. "Plenty of paraffin-covered matches in these watertight containers. A small ax? It's a little heavier than a hatchet, but it will be a lot more useful when your boyfriend starts chopping wood."

"I'll be doing the chopping, too," Cleo said.

"Well, of course." He showed her a folding army shovel. "Good for a lot of things. You could use it to chop as well as dig."

Chop what? she thought, but just nodded okay, she'd take it.

"Now, here's something I recommend to every-one. *The Wild Foods Trail Book.*"

"What do I need that for?"

"Well, you never know. Supposing your canoe tips over and your supplies are lost, and you're on your own in the bush. What would you do about food?"

"I don't know."

He tapped the book. "You could just refer to this and find yourself all sorts of goodies and free-bies."

"Okay, throw it in," she said, not even catching on till later that if she lost all her supplies in the lake she'd lose the book, too. He filled the knap-sack as they went along. "A length of rope," he said. "This one's twenty-five feet. Rope comes in handy if you have to throw up a shelter or need an emergency anchor."

"Anchor a boat with a rope?" she said.

"No, no, you could tie it around a rock, do you see?"

"Oh, sure, of course." He must think she was the world's dumbest camper. But she felt by the way he was smiling at her that it wasn't true. He was very sweet and really patient.

"What about food? We mustn't forget food."

No, mustn't forget food. Fatso needs her food. Won't be any handy restaurants where she's going. "What do you have?" she said.

"Everything." He showed her the shelves of dry foods, neat foil-and-plastic packages. Meal-size servings for two. Stewed beef, spaghetti sauce and meatballs, chicken with mushrooms, and even exotic meals like curried shrimp and scallopini with tarragon. There were packets of rice pudding, cocoa mix, powdered eggs and bacon, and a mixture of nuts, chocolate, and raisins that the salesman called Trail Mix. "It's just like Indian pemmican," he said.

"With chocolate?" Cleo said.

"There's a difference, but it serves the same purpose—a compact and high-energy food."

He threw in a dozen packets, then at her nod another dozen. "And that, and that, and that," she said pointing.

Glenn looked at the pile of food she'd accumulated. "That's a lot of good eating."

"My boyfriend eats a lot," she said quickly. And so does somebody else we know. Somebody else has bought enough food for two fat people, and that somebody else is going to eat it all by herself. "What else do I need?"

"Fishing gear? It's always nice to catch some fresh fish for supper. And a knife to clean the fish." He showed her a sheathed six-inch knife with a stout blade. "This is the one I use myself."

Cleo touched the blade. "Sharp."

"It's no toy, but it's just the ticket for the bush."

The knapsack bulged. He hooked the ax and sleeping bag on the outside of the frame. "Well, I guess that about does it." He added up the charges. It came to several hundred dollars. He looked up. "Better check that again, eh?"

"No, that's all right." She dug into her overalls and handed him four one-hundred-dollar bills. He looked flustered. Maybe she should have let him add up the bill twice. That's right, Rich and Dumb, most people don't go around with hundred-dollar bills in their overalls.

"Would you wait just one minute, please," he said, and hurried off. Cleo stuffed her small orange knapsack into the big one. In a few minutes Glenn was back with her change and the bill. "Would you mind signing here?" Before she thought, she had signed her name. Cleo Murphy. He looked at it. "Fine, Cleo. I envy you and your boyfriend getting off into the wilderness. I wish I had the time, I'd go with you." Smiling, he raised the pack to her back.

Cleo was unprepared for the weight. The straps cut into her shoulders. What had he sold her? She could hardly move. He escorted her to the door and held it open for her. "Well, bon voyage."

"Good-bye. Thank you." The pack hurt so much she was almost in tears. She went only a block and she had to stop and rest.

In a drugstore she bought a few more things she'd thought of—soap, tampons, toothbrush, toothpaste, and shampoo, then caught a cab to take her to the bus station on Bay Street.

At the depot she bought a ticket for North Adams. This was the next-to-last step of her escape plan. From North Adams it was seven miles to the lake. Maybe she could find a cab in North Adams. And a chauffeured limo, as well.

Late in the afternoon she boarded the bus, and began an endless journey past fields, farms, and little towns: Barrie, Clayton, Gravenhurst, Stottsville, Dorset. She got off the bus only to use the bathroom and renew her supply of Swiss chocolate bars. Bored with the long hot trip, she started reading the book the salesman had sold her. Unbelievable stuff, telling people to eat dandelions and violets and all sorts of exotic things she'd never even heard of, but it was sort of interesting, too.

Dozing off, she dreamed she was on the island looking into the cabin. Jam was inside, but it was dark and Cleo couldn't see her clearly. She rapped on the window, but it was closed, so she ran to the door and pushed it open. . . .

The bus stopped, jolting Cleo awake. Two boys

got off. Was this her stop? It was dark outside. "Where are we?" she asked a man across the aisle.

"Parish," he said. "How far do you have to go yet?"

"North Adams."

"You've got a good ways to go still."

A man walked by with a child wrapped in his arms. She felt a pang. She was alone. Nobody would be waiting for her when she arrived in North Adams, and certainly not on the island. Only the island waited. The island and the cabin. She was in a strange state—tired, but elated, too. She had come so far, so quickly, into another country with strangers all around her.

It was late, nearly midnight, when the bus pulled into North Adams. She left the book on the seat along with a bunch of crumpled chocolate wrappers. North Adams was one long, dark, empty street, the stores closed, only a single light at the crossroads.

One other person got off, a gray-haired woman who crossed the street and hurried away. So this was North Adams. Cleo had never been here before. All the other times they'd flown in on float planes and landed on the lake. The driver pulled her knapsack from the storage section and tossed it on the sidewalk. "Somebody picking you up?"

Cleo looked up the street as if she expected

someone momentarily. "Which way is the lake?" she asked the driver. He pointed up the road. She dragged the knapsack to the side of a building. When the bus left she worked her arms through the straps, heaved the sack onto her back, and began walking. By the time she got to the edge of town she was dripping with sweat. The dirt road was dark and deserted. Overhead the sky was clouded, with just a few stars. Why hadn't she thought to carry her flashlight? It was somewhere down in the bottom of the knapsack.

Gradually her eyes got accustomed to the darkness. She saw the shape of the split-wood fences along the road, the dim patches of overgrown fields, and the long stretches of dark woods. There's nobody out here. Animals, maybe, but they aren't going to hurt you. Only people hurt you, and there are no people.

She walked, the only sound the steady crunch of her feet. She thought she must be getting close to Dundee, but at a crossroads the sign said eight kilometers to Big Clear Lake.

A car came up behind her, the headlights flowing through the trees. She dropped off the shoulder of the road and crouched there, waiting for the car to pass. It was hard to get back to her feet. The straps rubbed her shoulders raw.

Eight kilometers—it should be easy. It would

have been easy for a normal human being. She passed a tiny hamlet of dark, unlit houses, makeshift fences, old cars in the yards. A dog came barking out at her. She ran, the knapsack bouncing on her back, lost her footing, and fell, then just lay there. . . .

Come on, fatso, on your feet. If Frank Garrity finds you, he'll ship you back express to your father.

She pulled herself up. She could just hear her grandmother. "Have you gone mad, Cleo? Wandering around Canada in the middle of the night. Do you even know what you're doing?"

For a while she dragged the knapsack along the road on its aluminum frame. Then she put it up on her back again. Blisters formed on the soles of her feet.

It was nearly morning when she reached the closed fieldstone and iron gates of Dundee. She hobbled past the gates, through the woods, circling around the tennis courts and the putting green white with early-morning dew. She stayed far away from Frank's cottage and his two dogs.

Her father owned everything on this end of the lake. Nobody else lived here. Miles of uninhabited forest, thick dark forests of spruce, wild, uncontrolled, without end or limit. Duck Island was his, too, out there somewhere in the middle of the water. The birds started to sing when she reached the boathouse. It was still half dark, maybe another hour to dawn. There, in front of her, was the silver, leaden surface of the lake—cold, dark, and still. It frightened her. All that water she had to cross to get to the island.

# Chapter 5

Cleo dropped her knapsack, then stood for a moment rubbing her shoulders. She was here at the lake just as she'd imagined, but it was like a dream. *You're here. . . . You're really here. . . .*

A motorboat was tied up by the dock—it might have been the same boat in which Frank had taken her and Jam to the island. Simple enough to start it, but it would be a stupid thing to do. Even if she got away, Frank would know someone was on the lake. That one last step of her escape plan —crossing from Dundee to the island—had seemed like such a tiny step. That time with Frank it couldn't have taken more than twenty minutes in the motorboat. They'd gone along the shore east of Dundee until they came to the point, then Frank had turned the boat sharply and gone straight across the water. "Straight across," he'd yelled above the sound of the motor. She had imagined she would cross as easily as that.

Sitting on her knapsack, she stared dimly out over the expanse of water. What now? She was so tired . . . too tired to think . . . ready to quit. The sky was getting lighter. There was a double row of green canoes racked up beside the boathouse, but no paddles. Frank kept them locked inside the boathouse, the key up on the rafters, but she didn't care where the key was, or the paddles. She didn't want a canoe. The thought of doing anything physical almost made her sick. Hadn't she done enough?

Beautiful, Cleo. Just sit there and wait for Frank to come and take you across to the island. That's the way to do it, Miss Rich, Dumb, and Lazy.

Okay, okay! That inner voice—how she hated it. She got to her feet, stood on a chair, and found the key. Inside the boathouse she took a paddle, then locked the door again and put the key back. From the back of the rack she took the lowest canoe, the one least likely to be missed, pushed it into the water, then climbed in. She could hardly hold the paddle straight. Behind her she saw the first light reflected in Dundee's many windows. Was someone standing at a window, watching her?

In a panic, she began to paddle, and didn't stop till she rounded the point and was out of sight of Dundee. Then she slumped and let the canoe drift. Everything ached, her back, shoulders, and arms. She wasn't used to using her body this hard. Face it, she wasn't used to using her body, period.

She must have slept, dropped off kneeling there in the canoe, because when she looked up the sun was sitting on the treetops, big, red, and angry-looking. The trees and the whole surface of the lake were on fire. . . . Streams of red ran across the water, as if the world itself were on fire, and this was the end.

Fighting her lethargy, she paddled away from the shore the way she remembered Frank turning the motorboat—the sun in her left eye. Waves splashed up across the bow, and she had trouble holding the canoe on course. She didn't think she was making any headway, but when she looked back the shore had receded. Tired again, she slapped the paddle down on the water and hit the side of the canoe.

Did she really remember the directions? It had been so long ago. The island, by itself in the middle of the lake, would be easy to miss. Beyond it, the lake stretched for miles. Was she past the island already, heading down the lake? Frightened, unsure, she stopped paddling. The wind whistled in her ears. Overhead a dark wedge òf clouds had spread across the sky. The canoe rode up and down on the swells. Up and down . . . up and down . . .

She began crying. That wasn't her. She never cried easily, but she was crying now. The world around her was so enormous . . . the sky . . . and the clouds hanging heavily overhead . . . and all this water. . . . She wasn't used to nature this way. There was too much of it. Nature was a park, or being with Jam away from everyone. Nature was a place to make believe, where she could imagine herself living in a tree. Not this endless world swallowing her up. She would have turned back. She was ready to turn back, but she didn't know which way to turn.

She had gone out on the lake as if she knew what she was doing. Wrong, wrong, wrong. She didn't know. She was going to die out here. "You brought it on yourself." Her grandmother's voice again. "Cleo, what am I going to do with you? You're so utterly incompetent, and sullen besides."

She found the package of trail food and took a mouthful, going down into that old foul mood where she hated herself and everything she did, and only wanted something comforting to put in her mouth. She chewed, swallowed, reached for another mouthful, sat there and ate while the

**40**

wind swung the canoe in circles. That was the way they'd find her on the lake—dead, but fat as a pig.

She paddled again. She had lost all sense of direction. Thick clouds covered the sky. No sun in her left eye now. When the clouds parted for a moment, the sun was high over head. The morning had passed. Where was she? Where was the island?

A rush of wings. A pair of loons flew overhead, their wild cries sending shivers through her. They disappeared quickly, and she was alone again. Paddling . . . paddling . . . nothing but water and sky . . .

When she first saw the island she didn't understand what she was looking at. It was over to her left, something raised up above the water. She thought it was a mirage, that she was seeing things, seeing what she wanted to see. She paddled toward it, not believing. Anyway, it didn't look like an island. It looked like a green raft. And then, as she drew closer, it looked like a lot of trees floating on the water. Closer still, and she saw rocks and bushes and the way it humped up in the middle. It had to be the island. Duck Island. Her island.

# Chapter 6

Rain spattered across the water. Only moments before, Cleo's arms had felt as if they were coming out of their sockets, but now she paddled vigorously, looking for the cabin on the island. The shoreline was mostly woods and swamp and steep banks. Ducks flew into the air. The rain came down harder. Soon, in just a few more minutes, she'd be inside the cabin, dry, warming herself by the fire she'd build in the stove.

She shouted when she saw the beach, then drove the canoe toward it. Her beach! Ten strokes . . . fifteen . . . sixteen . . . she couldn't wait to get to shore. Kicking off her boots she splashed into the water. I'm here, Jam. I did it. You knew I would, didn't you? She smelled evergreens and the heat rising from the wet rocks.

She scrambled up the myrtle-covered slope to where the cabin stood on a knoll. She caught a whiff of wet ashes. Something was terribly wrong. The clearing was there but the cabin was gone.

She stood in the rain. After a while she moved under a tree. Her shirt stuck to her skin. She couldn't think—didn't want to think. The cabin was burned down. She blamed them—her grandmother, and Mrs. Terrero, and the cook, and Paula, the nurse who used to pull her hair when she combed it. "Where are you all? What did you do it for? Why have you left me here?" She beat her fists on her thighs and screamed.

"I hope you all die."

Even as she was screaming she knew she should stop. There was nobody to blame. Shivering, she dragged her knapsack under a tree and got out her poncho, then something to eat, marmalade in a plastic bag . . . dipped her fingers in and ate till her teeth ached.

The rain spattered across the sand. She tipped the canoe over and crawled underneath, but the rain and wind drove her out. In the woods, branches hit her in the face and water dripped down her neck. Climbing over a fallen tree she slipped and scraped her elbow. She was going up a hill. There were rocks . . . big fat slabs that had slid down. She found one that she could get under, and lay with her knees pulled in against her chest, her hands between her legs. She couldn't stop shivering.

Sleep came. She dreamed about clouds . . . thick soft white clouds covering her completely except for her head. And all around, other heads were stuck in the clouds like lollipops. "This is the perfect way to live," she said.

When she woke she heard the wind rushing through the trees. It was night, blacker than anything she'd ever known in her life. No light, no break in an impenetrable wall of darkness. She had stopped shivering. Her clothes were sodden, but she'd heated up in the rubber poncho. Her eyes closed heavily. Sleep . . . sleep . . . wake up somewhere else. . . . She heard something—a sniffling, snuffling noise, and nails striking rock. An animal was out there, so close she smelled it, rank and overpowering like rotten fish.

She backed under the rock till she couldn't back any further. When she felt its soft tiny fingers on her face, she screamed, then heard it scramble away through the leaves.

She was afraid to close her eyes. Had she come here to die? Was that what her flight meant? Was that why she was under this rock—to die here, to join Jam and her mother?

Jam, where are you? Why am I here alone?

Why aren't you here with me! Why did you die? You had no right to die!

She felt the darkness separating. . . . A figure came out of the darkness . . . part of the darkness . . . like the darkness itself . . . a woman, shrouded in mourning, her face hidden. "Mother? Is that you, Mother? Are you coming for me?" Cleo wanted to be taken. Take me away. . . . Take me with you. . . .

The sky grew light. She had died that night. Not forever. Not for the last time. There were so many ways to die. She had died every time she was sent away to school . . . every time she had to leave Jam . . . when her mother died . . . and now . . . now . . .

Wet, gloomy woods. Cleo felt sick, every bone in her body ached. She crawled out from under the rock, took off her poncho and overalls, and squatted. All around her were trees and rocks and dead trees and moss and ferns. She felt mean, stupid, and scared. These trees, these woods—she hated them . . . told herself she wasn't lost, but felt lost. She started walking.

Every branch she touched cascaded water. Briars caught her poncho. She plunged blindly through tangles of bushes, came out steaming, scratched, and bleeding.

In a thick clump of evergreens birds exploded in

her face, then disappeared in an instant. Past the evergreens the lake shone below her, and almost at her feet was the beach, her canoe pulled up on shore, just where she'd left it.

She emptied her knapsack on the ground, dug through the packets of food, and found the Trail Mix. She hadn't eaten since the day before. It was a wonder she was even alive. How had Big Belly survived? Bless the goop. Food changed her mood. She leaned back against a rock, for the first time let herself look around, sniff, and listen. The rock was warm against her back, the silence so thick she could almost feel it, and the water was like a million diamonds.

She was here, really here, not in a dream, not wanting, or wishing. . . . She was on the island, alone, not a soul on the lake, no voices, no motors, alone. . . .

Three days on her own, and she was still alive. For the first time in her life she'd really done something, gotten someplace by herself without anyone's help, without directors, or counselors, or instructors hanging over her.

Yes, you've really done it. The no voice jumped in. Landed yourself on a wild empty island with no shelter, no place to sleep. What are you going to do now, Marvelous Murphy?

"Not listen to you, bigmouth!"

She'd stay one more day. The sky had cleared. It probably wouldn't rain. Bees and dragonflies buzzed around. It was so peaceful she fell asleep. A vicious sting on the leg woke her. She swatted at a big, hairy horsefly.

The sun was high and hot. She emptied the knapsack and put things out to dry and discovered she had forgotten a bathing suit. Took off her overalls and T-shirt—hard for her to accept herself naked. In the showers at school she always had a big towel handy, never looked at herself in a mirror like some of the girls. Her face was all right. She could look at her face a lot, and she didn't really mind her breasts and arms, but when she thought of her body—that big soft white belly —it reminded her of the old stone earth goddesses, little fat fertility figures with big sagging breasts, round bellies, and fat thighs. That was her, except her breasts didn't sag. . . . Still, it was nice taking off her clothes and feeling the wind on her skin.

The water was cold, green, and clear. Dead trees lay on the bottom. She dived down, then surfaced and swam hard. Swimming was the one thing she did well. In the water nobody could see her except for her head, but on a tennis court, or riding a horse, she felt everyone's eyes on her big butt.

She dried herself, then put on her overalls. Hungry again. That was the trouble with exercise—it made her want to eat twice as much. She started to eat more goop, then thought she'd better fix a place to sleep before the sun went down. Above the beach she tied a rope between two trees and threw the poncho over it. It looked like a tent. There was just enough room underneath for her sleeping bag.

She glanced at her watch again—really compulsive about the time, looking at her watch every few minutes. Where was she going? What difference did it make what time it was? How else are you going to know when supper is served, stupid?

The afternoon slipped away. Shadows lay across the beach. She gathered wood and twigs, found the matches dry, in their plastic case. The fire flared up, and she felt proud. She got water in the collapsible pail. Now she was glad she'd brought all that stuff. What if she'd come with nothing, expecting to find everything in the cabin?

She boiled water and threw in one of the packages of vegetable soup, ate every drop, and was still hungry.

She sat on a rock looking out over the water—at her side, jelly in a little plastic case and a box of crackers. Broad curving currents meandered across the surface, swallows swooped over the water, waves licked at the shore. It was quiet and peaceful. There was nothing she had to do, no one she had to get ready for, no special way she had to dress or be. She ate the crackers and jelly slowly, virtuously. She wasn't gobbling her food the way her grandmother always accused her. She nibbled the crackers like a lady, then licked the jelly from her fingers. Sorry, Grandmother!

At dark she crawled into her makeshift tent, lay on her back, and watched the stars appear in the sky. She was tired, but contented. She knew she wanted to stay on the island.

"Jam," she whispered. She felt her sister's presence, had felt it ever since she came to the island. Jam was here, no place else.

# Chapter 7

Cleo staggered up, dazed from the heat, and fell into the water with her clothes on. The poncho had come loose during the night, and the morning sun had baked into her. The water was like cool cream, took the ache out of her arms and legs. She decided to stay in forever. The water rocked her gently. . . . The trees and the sky glistened through her wet lashes. If only the cabin still stood on the knoll, everything would be so simple.

She flopped over, floated face down, arms outspread, her shadow big beneath her. A school of shining minnows flashed by. The sun was high overhead. Noon already and nothing done. Just dreaming. She hadn't even eaten. Well, that wasn't so bad. What should she do? Go back? Stay? Go back home . . . to camp . . . to school. . . . Without

Jam, it was all nothing. When she thought of her father and grandmother she felt nothing . . . emptiness. She turned over, floated on her back.

Look at her *now*. In the water with her clothes on! Cleo could hear their voices—her grandmother, her teachers, her instructors. What's the matter with her? She's indifferent. Lazy, I say! Lacks initiative. A lackadaisical character. If she doesn't pull herself together, she'll never amount to anything!

Lackadaisical was right. She was inert. A floating zombie. Come on, make a decision. Are you going to stay on the island? Or are you going to go?

"How can I stay?" she said out loud. "The cabin is gone."

Sleep on the beach. You did it last night.

"And what do I do if it rains?" Besides, she was right out in plain sight here if anybody came by in a motorboat. It could be Frank Garrity patrolling the waters, looking for the missing canoe. Her stomach jumped. From Frank to her father—one little phone call. That would be it. She could see her father dropping from the sky in a helicopter and snatching her away.

She stood in the water and looked up at the sky. Clear blue around her, but to the south there was a spreading white haze. Was it going to rain again? It always rains, the no voice told her glee-fully. You'll have to go back . . . like a dog drag-ging its tail.

She clumped out of the lake and stood irreso-lutely, then changed into overalls and a yellow shirt. No, she wasn't going back. Couldn't. No. No, no, NO. She'd find something for shelter. Robinson Crusoe didn't have a cabin waiting for *him* when he was shipwrecked. He'd built one. That's what she should do. Lady Murphy is going to build a cabin? Tell me another one! Okay, a lean-to. Two walls and a roof to keep the rain off. Chop down a few trees and hook them together somehow. She went into the woods, picked out a small tree, and started chopping. She didn't know how to use an ax. The tree bounced every time she hit it. She stopped to catch her breath. She'd hardly made a mark on the tree.

Throwing down the ax, she went back to the beach and sat on a rock, eyes shut against the glare from the lake.

Told you you couldn't build anything, the no voice jeered.

"I'll find a rock to sleep under."

Is that what you call a sensible idea?

"I just need a place to be dry!"

And what about the animals?

"Shut up! Shut up!" She didn't know what she'd

do, but there was something in her that wouldn't let go. A stubborn streak. Her stupid streak, her grandmother would call it. She jumped up, sick of worrying what her grandmother thought. For once in her life she was going to do something the way she wanted to. Her ideas, her decisions, her mistakes!

She had to find someplace to hide the canoe so it couldn't be seen from the lake. She rolled up the sleeping bag and ground cloth, loaded the canoe, and pushed off. She was going to stay. Then she said it aloud. *"I'm going to stay."* A hiding place for the canoe first, then some kind of shelter from the rain, like that rock where she'd slept the first night, only better—a lot better. As she drifted away from the shore, she looked back at the beach, saw the remains of her fire, the two trees where she'd strung the ground cloth, and the hollowed-out place where she'd slept. It wasn't much, but it was hers, something she'd created with her own hands. When she was little she was never allowed to do things. There was always someone else there—Mrs. Terrero, the housekeeper, and the cook, and the nurses—other hands, quicker, more skilled than hers, pushing her hands aside, doing things faster and better. *You go and play now.*

She knew nothing about real life, what real

people did. Whatever she knew she had learned from reading. She used to dream about what she would do if they were poor, if her father wasn't her father, and there were just her mother, Jam, and herself together, living in a few rooms, and terribly poor. She would go out and work, bring home money. They'd be poor, but the three of them would be together and happy. Happy—it was such a strange word. She could never tell what would make her happy, only knew afterwards, like that last day with Jam, when she'd yelled down from the window. She'd been happy that day. She knew it now.

Paddling slowly in the shadow of the island, she saw the trees and the sky reflected in the water . . . herself in between, not in one world or the other. The shoreline was rocky, overgrown with shrubs and trees. No place to hide the canoe. She ought to have gone the other way. The day would go and she'd still be on the water. Just as she was thinking about turning back she drifted into a glassy little inlet and saw three deer standing in the water.

She didn't know who was more startled, she or the deer. The largest one turned and almost soundlessly leaped through an opening in the hill. The two smaller deer followed. It was magical.

Where the deer had been, a stream emptied into the lake, its hidden opening littered with dead trees. She pulled the canoe over the top, but once on the other side she was afloat again, and paddled slowly up a long rocky corridor past shelves of rock filled with plants and flowers. The air vibrated with the sounds of insects and birds.

An animal with a sleek head swam past. Birds crossed back and forth ahead of her. Clouds of insects followed her as she guided the canoe around sandbars and through gravel-bottomed pools. When she couldn't follow the stream any further she tied the canoe to a tree overhanging the bank.

She left everything in the canoe and started climbing the rocky ledges. A hot, tiring climb. The air was full of little gnats that flew into her ears and eyes. The rocks were like big steps going up the hill. She poked around them, looking for an opening, a shelter, dry and safe from animals. She moved from rock to rock climbing higher and higher, till she reached the top of the island. She was hot and sticky and discouraged. A big weathered oak stood alone, its long sloping arms touching the ground. Cautiously, she climbed along one of the low limbs, saw the lake through the trees, and climbed down.

Tomorrow you go back.

Go back. She hated the words, hated what they meant. She sat in the shade, brushing at the gnats, waiting for her fairy godmother to turn the pumpkin into a princess, turn a rock into a cabin, or a tree into a hut.

When she started back down she didn't look where she was going and found herself in the middle of a wet meadow choked with reeds and cattails. She didn't remember coming this way. Frogs splashed, mud sucked at her boots. A trickle of water meandered through the grass down a rocky incline and dropped into a little pool. Cleo slid down the hill and splashed water over her hot face, then lay there beside the pool, cooling off.

After a while she noticed an opening at the base of the hill and went over to take a look. The opening was low in the rocks and she had to bend down to look. Cool air washed over her face. Darkness . . . the musty smell of leaves and earth . . . and something else that made her back off.

She sat down and waited for whatever was in the cave to come out. But when nothing happened, she got impatient, found a long branch and poked it cautiously inside. "Hello? Anybody home?" She poked the branch around, then crawled in.

She couldn't see anything at first, and the musky odor reminded her of hyenas at the zoo. When she looked out the opening, she saw the pool, grass, trees, like a picture. The sounds from outside were muffled. It was strange being enclosed this way.

She wasn't sure she liked it, but if the animal who belonged here didn't return, she'd use it.

The cave was higher in back than in front and she could sit up. It was smaller than her closet at home, but big enough for her to lie down in. The floor of the cave was covered with dry little pellets that she brushed out along with the leaves and litter. If whoever lived here came back, he'd know he'd been moved out. Someone else was going to live here now.

When she crawled out the sun was going down. She climbed up to the wet meadow, and lost sight of the cave. Afraid she wouldn't be able to find her way back, she pulled off her yellow shirt, tied it to a branch, then started down. When she looked back the shirt stood out like a flag. She made a pile of rocks for a marker and went on, marking her trail all the way down to the stream. At the canoe, she took her sleeping bag, a packet of trail food, and started back. She was tired, her feet kept going off the trail, and once she walked right into a tree.

It was really getting dark. There were moments when she didn't think she would find the cave. When she finally saw her yellow shirt she stood there panting like a dog. At the cave she didn't have the strength to do anything but unroll the sleeping bag and climb in.

She lay with her head outside the cave and saw

the shadows of night birds swooping for insects. The sound of the water splashing into the pool comforted her.

High above in the soft, dark sky she saw the first star. Jam would have loved it here, she thought. Tears filled her eyes. A whip-poor-will chattered in the woods. Whip . . . poor . . . *will* . . . whip . . . poor . . . *will* . . . whip . . . poor . . . *will*. . . . Each time the bird cried, she heard it say never*beee*. . . . Never*beee* . . . never*beee* . . . Listening, she fell asleep to its call.

# Chapter 8

A crackling noise in the woods made Cleo look around. A little burst of sound, then silence. It was a gray, still morning, and she was squatting over a shallow toilet hole she had scooped out. The mosquitoes were bad. The crackling started again. A copper-colored chipmunk poked through the leaves. "Hello," she said, hoping he'd come close. He sat on a stump and looked at her sideways. In her overalls pocket she found some nuts left over from the Trail Mix and, making a little chipping noise, called him to her. "You're pretty," she said. He was a sleek little creature with long stripes down his back. She threw him a nut. He darted away, then circled back, sniffed it out, then turned it a couple of times before popping it into his mouth.

She threw another nut, a little nearer this time.

He hesitated, then darted forward. There was a distinct white scar across his nose. "You look like Al Capone." Her voice sent him scurrying. This time he didn't return.

She swatted a mosquito. Horrible little blood-sucking vampires wouldn't let her be. They bothered her all the way down to the canoe, where she got her knapsack and started back. It was okay when she was moving, but every time she paused she heard the mosquitoes circling around her head.

As the sun came up the mosquitoes relented, and she thought of all the things she had to do. Out of habit she glanced at her watch. She told herself, Do the first thing, and when that's finished, the second. That was how she had gotten this far. Work on the cave, then the fire, and third, food. Deliberately she put food last. It was food she wanted first, but she hated that appetite in herself. She wanted to control it, not let it control her.

Cleaning rocks and debris away from the entrance of the cave, she discovered that the entrance was bigger than she'd thought at first, nearly a foot higher, and wider, too. Instead of having to crawl in on all fours, she could stoop and go in and out.

The work had tired her out and she sat down to rest. Her stomach was crying, but she wasn't ready to feed it yet. She was thinking about a broom. She'd swept the cave out once on her hands and knees, didn't want to do that again. Too bad that cute little guy at the Toronto store, that Glenn, hadn't thought to send her out with a broom. He'd thought of just about everything else. Well, she couldn't go running back to him now. The first thing she tried was close at hand, little bunched pine needles that looked like miniature brooms, but were too soft for the cave's rough floor. She found something stiffer, long brushy branches that she tied together with a piece of string. Crude, but it worked.

There was a ledge along one wall of the cave, not very wide, but big enough for a bed. She piled armfuls of pine needles and evergreen boughs almost to the ceiling, then put her sleeping bag on top and sank down into it. It was like a nest, soft and sweet-smelling, dim and snug. She liked it so much she fell asleep.

She woke refreshed, felt good with the rock walls around her, as if she were in her own place. In every school and every camp she'd attended she'd always had that need—to know what was hers, which bed, which corner.

She was now so hungry she made quick work of the fireplace. A circle of stones in front of the cave, then a fire of pine needles, dry twigs, and branches. She dumped a package of chicken and rice curry into a pot, then set it on the coals. While it was cooking, she looked around for a place to hang her knapsack and pots. A pine tree close by with its ring of stubby dead branches worked perfectly.

Too late, she smelled something burning. She snatched the pot off the fire, then sat on the ground eating the charred food. She was so hungry anything would have tasted good. Al Capone, the bold chipmunk, returned and she threw him the burnt parts of the meal. So nothing went to waste.

After she finished eating she washed her socks, underwear, and dirty overalls in the pool, then threw them over bushes in the sun. Barefoot, she moved around gingerly.

Later, before going down to the lake she divided the packets of food into groups of three—breakfast, lunch, and supper—then laid them out in rows across a rock. Three meals a day would give her twenty-eight days on the island. But if she ate only twice a day, she could stay forty-two days. That would take her into the middle of August. And why not two meals a day? The less she ate, the better she felt about herself. But could she do it? The way she had made herself wait for breakfast this morning had been pure torture. She decided to eat only two packaged meals a day.

The only extras allowed would be things like berries, which she'd seen growing everywhere, and any fish she caught.

She took the fishing pole, laced her boots together over her shoulders—she'd go as far as she could barefoot—then went straight down toward the water, again marking her trail with rocks. She stopped often to pick raspberries.

She swam and then fished. She'd always liked fishing in the different camps she'd attended, dropping her line into the water and waiting, never knowing what her line would bring up. She cast off the rocks with her fishing lure—a little red and white spoon—but didn't catch anything.

On her way back she filled the pockets of her overalls with berries. At the cave she got involved figuring out a way to make a real fireplace. Using a boulder near the cave as a back she built up the sides with small stones. It was late when she finished and she was hungry again. She dragged a log over for a seat, then started a fire. She emptied a package of instant oatmeal and raisins into boiling water. Curry for breakfast and oatmeal for supper. Her grandmother would love that. She ate from the pot again, then, still hungry, remembered the berries. They were crushed in her pocket. What a mess. She ate what she could, licking her fingers.

That night as she lay on her high fragrant bed,

head covered against the mosquitoes, she dropped right off to sleep. Later she woke up, didn't know where she was. Everything was cut loose . . . blackness . . . no sense of herself . . . was she awake, or dreaming? Turn on the light, please!

She reached for her flashlight, shone it around the walls and through the opening. There was nobody here, no lights, no houses, no human sounds. How far she'd come from the world! She felt alone, so desperately alone.

# Chapter 9

The rain came unexpectedly. Only minutes before the sun had been shining and Cleo was on her way down to swim. The insects were all around her, in her eyes and mouth, not biting, but annoying. Then it started to rain. She ran back to the cave, grabbed everything outside and threw it inside, then ducked in herself, only failed to duck low enough and hit her head. It put her into a foul mood. She sank down on her sack with all the damp clothes.

Four days in the cave, and everything still was so hard. Would she ever get used to it? No tables, no bureaus, no closets or shelves, everything on the ground: the wood, the fire, her clothes. At the end of every day she felt as if she had weights on her arms and legs. She was good for an hour or two in the morning, but then all she wanted to do was sleep or eat. That was what she wanted now, something sweet on her tongue. Too early for dinner. For four days she had successfully kept to two meals a day. Maybe it was not eating that was making her so weak and leaden-limbed all the time.

Lying on the sleeping bag, she thought about home, about her father and her grandmother. Had they missed her yet? It seemed so long ago. Hardly a week, and already that other life was so distant. Was it possible they didn't know? And what would they do when they found out? Would they think she was dead, too? Would they be sorry? Feel bad? It made her feel bad for them. She might have called them, or written, told them she was going away but that she was all right. There was nothing she could do about it now. Too risky to canoe to the mainland. Frank had probably missed the canoe by now, and would be looking for it. Someone else might recognize her. Even if she got to town unobserved, what would she do? Letters were postmarked, and could be traced. Rain continued steadily, sheets of rain. Everything was trying to get out of the wet. The insects hid under the leaves, the birds disappeared, she had crawled into a hole, and so had the chipmunks and squirrels.

Her eyelids closed. She resisted, didn't want to sleep all the time. Think about that cute salesman in Toronto. Glenn. He'd been so sympathetic. It had been his eyes . . . so dark, and warm and alive. Had he liked her? He must have, because he'd been so nice to her, and said he wished he could go with her.

Said it just to please you, Dumbo. Because you were a customer spending a bundle.

She didn't want to think so. He was too good-looking to have to bother impressing her. Dumb of her to have said she had a boyfriend. Why hadn't she said she was going alone? *How about the two of us teaming up?* Yes, he'd say. I wouldn't mind.

Now what if he were here, right now, in the cave with her? The thought warmed her all over; a glow, a really good feeling spread through her whole body.

The rain was still coming down heavily when she woke. She was going to have to spend the day here. She thought idly about building a fire in the entrance, but it seemed like too much work. She had to urinate, but she didn't feel like doing that, either. Maybe she'd never do anything.

She looked at the clothes strewn around. If only she had some hooks. It was really simple once she thought about it—wedge a branch into one of the cracks in the wall. A good thought like that woke her right up. She sat up and hit her head again. Oh, nuts! She'd never learn!

But she had learned something. Using a rock as a hammer she found several places to wedge pegs into the walls, and she was able to hang up all her clothes. It was these little things that made life better: driving pegs into a wall, learning to air her sleeping bag every day to keep it smelling fresh, and finally using the ax properly, getting it high over her head and then bringing it down on the wood clean and sharp. Angle left, angle right . . . chipping away at a log till it looked like a tree the beaver gnawed down along the waterway.

By the end of that first week in the cave, the leaden feeling, the need to sleep all the time, had lifted. She was still slow, but she was doing things. Going everywhere barefoot. She really admired her bare, dirty feet! When had she ever had dirty feet before?

Everything she did for herself built her confidence. In the morning she was up with the birds, who were everywhere. Almost every day she returned to the oak tree on top of the island, climbing a little higher each time. And she was controlling her eating—no more than two meals a day.

Before breakfast, she went off on brief expeditions, following her old trail to the stream where the canoe was tied up, or making new trails to the shallows at the western end of the island, where she sometimes saw the deer. She still marked her trails, but more and more she noticed prominent trees, a mass of rock, or the way the land rose and fell.

One morning before breakfast she went back to the burned-down cabin. In the ruins she found a dented enamel pan, a mason jar, and several forks with long, old-fashioned tines. At the cave she set the pan in a niche high in a rock, hung a towel nearby on a branch, set her soap on the stone, and put her toothbrush into the mason jar. A perfect washstand. She immediately filled the pan and gave herself the pleasure of washing standing up.

That morning she made pancakes. The chipmunks appeared the moment she poured the mix into the hot pan. They had been thriving on her burned food. She recognized a number of chipmunks now—one had a ratty tail, another a chewed ear. Old scarface, Al Capone, was her favorite. He didn't let the other chipmunks forget this was his territory, and was kept busy driving them away, then hurrying back to see if she'd burned anything yet.

"Not today, Al. This one is going to be perfect." She flipped the pancake over in time, then moved the pan to the edge of the fire while the other side cooked.

Everything was better. She even had her first unexpected night visitor and didn't panic. She heard something padding around outside the cave and reached for her flashlight. Maybe the real owner had returned to claim the cave. When she flashed on the light, she got a scare, thought it was a bear poking into her supper pot, but when he raised his snout and peered at her she saw that it was a raccoon. Her light didn't seem to bother him, and he went back to sniffing around the fire. Only when she yelled did he amble off.

She didn't feel hostile. The raccoon belonged to the island before she did, but she didn't want him around her supplies. She thought about bringing the knapsack into the cave, but it was zipped, so why worry?

Often she went to the top of the island and looked out over the lake. There, in that extraordinary emptiness and silence, she felt Jam's presence.

Jam was dead . . . dead. . . . Only words. What did they mean? How could her sister be dead when Cleo still heard her voice, caught glimpses of her in the trees? It was beyond understanding. How could people be dead that you felt in your deepest being were alive?

She climbed along the long sloping branch of the oak, then pulled herself up a couple more branches. She wedged herself in a notch and looked far out over the lake. It was a dream, the island was a dream, and her life here. . . . She was dreaming it all. . . . Maybe her life before was a dream, too. . . .

"Wouldn't that be perfect, Jam? If I'd dreamed the whole thing?"

Later that day she went fishing. She baited her line with red worms and drifted off the island. All she got were a lot of little nibbles. When she pulled in her line the hook was bare. "If there's anything I hate, it's a fish who thinks it's smarter than me." But then something took the hook, and she brought in a creamy fat green bass.

That night she sat by the fire later than usual. The land was dark around her. She had filled up on fish and curried rice, finishing off the meal with raspberries. She watched the stars appear one after another. Occasionally she heard an airplane pass high overhead, then saw its tiny flashing red lights. It made her feel how close, and yet how distant, the world was.

It was time for her to go in, but she lingered. The night wind through the woods was cool and spicy. She heard the night birds, the whip-poor-will and the owls. The owls made a soft lonely sound. Hoo . . . hooo . . . hoo hoo hooo. She cupped her hands and answered back. "Hooo . . .

hooo . . . hooo hooo hooo . . ." She felt happy. She'd had a good day, made pancakes success- fully, climbed a tree, feasted on a fish she'd caught herself. She sat there for a long time, her arms wrapped around her knees.

# Chapter 10

Later on, she came to think of those first few weeks after she'd found the cave as her Eden time. A paradise with bugs. She woke each morning with the sun breaking through the tops of the trees, welcomed by the morning sounds of birds. One call like a pipe, another like a whistle. The leaves of a tree rustled, and the bird appeared—a black and gold oriole. It piped again. There were long shadows in the woods, dew on every leaf.

Waking, there was always that moment of surprise, that shock of pleasure—she was here, living on the island, in a cave. Who would have thought it? Her schoolmates would be amazed. Most mornings at school she woke in a panic, sure that she'd overslept. Whatever house she had lived in, it was always bedlam, a frantic busy place with girls pounding by in the halls.

Here she did everything at her own pace. She rose eagerly, combed her hair, pulled on shorts and shirt. She went barefoot everywhere now. How different she felt. No false masks, no phoniness, no Cleo the sullen granddaughter, or the fat, uncooperative camper, or the vaguely smiling schoolgirl.

She swept the cave, freshened her bed. Everything had a place now—her clothes on the pegs, her flashlight in the niche near the bed, her money and watch in another niche. Today was a hot, sunny morning, the sky cloudless, almost white with heat, the lake wrinkled with light. In all this space, was there anything but the island, or anyone but Cleo? At times this thought diminished her, made her feel insignificant; more often it enlarged her—all this space flowing through her, lifting her till she felt almost majestic, the ruler of water, land, and sky.

She dove into the lake. That first plunge, cool water against hot skin, was exquisite. She slid down into the cool silent depths, touched a dead tree, then rose quickly to the light. She swam far along the shore, testing her stamina, then returned.

A black water snake sunned itself in a bush. A big, gray-blue heron flew silently over the trees. The frogs on the rocks blinked their golden eyes at Cleo, then plunged for the safety of the water. She amused herself seeing how many frogs she could catch, then kissed her little frog princes before releasing them.

Afterward she sat on a rock, her legs stretched out, her face turned to the sun. Eyes closed, she listened to the wind, a distant bird, the water tossing endlessly on the shore . . .

The sun lay heavy on her shoulders and breasts. She felt tight and alive, languid and soft at the same time. She had never felt this way before, so open, so aware, so unashamed of herself, her body. What would Glenn think if he saw her?

A sound, a distant hum she'd pushed aside, grew louder. She fingered the long white scratches on her legs. The noise couldn't be ignored. She thought at first it was an airplane, but the sound was on the water. She dressed hastily. In the distance she saw a black speck moving across the water. A boat was coming straight for the island.

She ran up the trail and hid. When the boat got closer she recognized Frank Garrity, the caretaker at Dundee. He drifted slowly around the island, scanning the shore with binoculars. Had he missed the canoe? Had her father sent him? Her mind raced. What had she left on the shore?

He made a complete circle of the island, then turned back the way he'd come, from the mainland.

It was already past noon and she still hadn't

eaten. She picked through her supplies. It was hard to concentrate. What if Frank came back for her, forced her to leave the island?

"Nobody is coming for you," she said aloud. "Nothing has changed. This is a warning not to get complacent."

Al Capone ran to her feet and sat up expectantly. She threw him some seeds. "You're greedy, Al."

She whistled softly, making a chickadee sound, then waited with more seeds in her open hand. There were two chickadees in the tree above her. Cleo decided they were girlfriends. The chunkier one dropped down till she was on a branch just over Cleo's head. She kept turning and looking at Cleo, and then quick as a flash she was on Cleo's hand, picked at the seed twice before she got what she wanted, and flew off.

In the afternoon Cleo went down to the shore. A log washed up on the beach caught her eye. She propped it against a tree. Upright, its knots and holes became a soldier standing guard. He had a blunt bashed nose, a crooked mouth, a single empty eye.

Cleo looked at him from various angles. "If you're going to be a soldier, look like one." She turned him so he faced the lake. "Now if anybody comes, soldier, you shoot."

That made her feel better, but when she took the canoe out on the lake she stayed close to the inlet, uneasy about Frank. She'd been lucky this time.

As she drifted along the shore she trailed a little red and white lure. Dragonflies swooped over the water. Suddenly something tugged sharply on the line. It was all she could do to hold the pole. She let line go and it went spinning out. The pole bent in half. She let go, then reeled in . . . then let go . . . then reeled in. . . . The fish broke water, a huge green monster. She held on to the pole with both hands and brought the fish to the side of the boat. Its fins rippled, the gills opened and closed. It came into the canoe, yellow eyes mad with rage. It leaped, thumped, banged against the sides. She knocked it down with the paddle. Twice it nearly leaped out of the boat. Finally it lay still, tangled in the line.

On shore she chopped off the head. She could scarcely get her hands around the fish. She gutted it and cleaned out the insides. It was full of half-digested minnows.

At the cave she built a fire, cut long, thick fillets, ate the fish as fast as it cooked. She ate until she couldn't stuff in another mouthful, then cooked the few fillets that remained, planning to eat them for breakfast.

In the morning she saw that an animal had raked through the ashes of the fire and eaten the remains of the fish. It had to be the raccoon's work. Disappointed, but not too upset, she went for the knapsack on the tree. Oatmeal for breakfast again. The knapsack was gone. All around the tree there was a trail of food. And across a rock she saw the robber's paw prints, each one perfectly outlined in flour. In a thicket of trees she found the empty knapsack.

# Chapter 11

Cleo had once seen a woodpecker crash headlong into one of the big picture windows at St. Ives and then just lie on the ground, slowly blinking its eyes, unable to raise its head. That was how dazed she felt when she saw what the raccoon had done to her food. She would have to go back now. And when she returned, humbled and defeated, she would read in her grandmother's eyes her failure, her ineptitude, her utter stupidity in believing that she could live on the island, or anywhere, by herself.

Slowly she began to pick up things. There was a little oatmeal left in a plastic bag, more on the ground. She scooped up what she could and poured it back, dirt and all. She crawled around, saving odds and ends of different dinners, bits of dried rice and shrimp, a chunk of beef stew, a few handfuls of spaghetti and meatballs. Two unopened packets of Trail Mix were still in the knapsack. Altogether she salvaged nearly a week's supply of food. She packed it into the knapsack and carried it with her everywhere that day.

That night she slept with the knapsack under her head, the flashlight and ax at her side. Several times she woke, sure that the raccoon had returned. It made her sick remembering what he'd done. He was forcing her to leave the island. Better to eat Mr. Raccoon and stay. His belly, after all, was full of her food. If he came again, she'd bash his head with the ax.

The next day she started thinking about staying, about another way to exist, living on fish and berries and apples. Maybe there were other things to eat on the island. She remembered the book about gathering wild foods she'd left on the bus. It said you could eat dandelions and milkweed blossoms and day lilies. Cattails and water lilies. She remembered because the thought of eating flowers had been so odd—and they were supposed to be good for you. The roots of plants, and nuts (well, everyone knew that), and twigs and the inner bark of some trees (birch she thought) could be made into tea and flour.

She found an unopened dandelion and tasted it.

It was good at first, then she got a bitter aftertaste and spit it out, afraid she'd poisoned herself. There definitely were poisonous plants. The book had warned against them. One part of a plant could be poisonous, the root, say, or the leaf, and the rest of it could be good. Like rhubarb—you could eat the stem, but the leaf was poisonous. How could she know, though? Did she dare to try anything she wasn't sure of?

She carried her knapsack and fishing pole down to the shore, fished with the lure for a while without success, then switched to worms and caught half a dozen sunfish—small, but she wasn't throwing anything back.

Later she went down to the stream and made her way slowly along the banks picking raspberries. It was hot, and the knapsack stuck to her back. She picked till her fingers were stained purple, then went looking for apples behind the ruins of the cabin. The deer had been there before her. Their tracks were under the trees, along with the apples they'd bitten into and left. There wasn't much to choose from—a lot of hard little green apples.

It was a nuisance carrying her knapsack everywhere. Not that much food remained, but what she had was precious and she was determined to keep it safe.

She thought about stoning off a part of the back of the cave as a storeroom but decided instead to dig into the sandy floor and make some kind of covered pit. The hole almost dug itself, but removing the sand and lining the pit with stone was hard work. Over the pit she set a heavy stone that the raccoon would never move—nor would she, very easily.

That night she ate only the fish and stewed apples and in the morning woke with real hunger pangs. She drove off Al Capone, who came sniffing around for nuts. "No handouts today!"

It started raining, a fine persistent drizzle. Cleo put on her poncho and went down to fish. Drifting along the island she trailed the red and white spoon. Rain dripped off her poncho. She reeled in, then cast out again. Her feet were wet, and she was chilled from sitting so long. She paddled to the beach. Off the point she baited her line with a worm. Something solid struck it immediately.

The fish broke water. She didn't play around with it, just reeled in, yanked it out of the water and grabbed it. A beautiful speckled green and white bass. She built a fire right on shore. The wood was damp, and the fire kept threatening to go out. The fish was in the embers, barely singed, when the rain suddenly came down hard.

Grabbing everything, she jumped back into the

canoe and paddled as fast as she could for the stream, where she ran the canoe under the shelter of the overhanging banks. The fish lay at her feet, black from the fire but still raw inside. She bit a little piece. It was like biting into rubber. The Japanese eat raw fish, she reminded herself, and so do the Eskimo.

Rain spattered into the stream. She bit into the fish again, chewed, and finally swallowed.

*Eating raw fish.* It was her grandmother's voice. *Pure savagery.*

Cleo grinned. "That's me, your dear savage granddaughter. That's my distinction. Cleo Murphy, the savage, who loves raw fish." She took another bite. It was almost as bad as the first one. Outside, there was a mist in the treetops. Inside, under the poncho, out of the wind and rain, she was beginning to steam. She chewed the fish slowly, then bit into another piece.

# Chapter 12

Cleo leaned forward, her hands over her belly, and burped. She was full, fuller than she'd been in days, but not happily full. She burped again, a loud, disgusting froglike burp.

Earlier she'd cooked a pot of dandelions, limp as spinach and bitter. She'd forced down a slimy mouthful, then another, then the whole mess, and now she felt gassy as an old balloon.

Dandelions were supposed to be safe. Was anything safe? Eat less, that was the key. The less she ate, the less danger of poisoning herself. The way she felt now, she might never eat again.

The following day, recovered and feeling normal, she was more optimistic, picked strawberry leaves and a grass that tasted like garlic. What she had to do with new foods was try a tiny bit at a time, then wait to see if it was good or bad.

Later, in the woods above the cave, she gathered dead pine branches and cones for her fire. The crows cawed in the trees, six or eight of them, flying at something high in a pine. A large bird fell erratically through the branches. The crows attacked, driving it down to the ground.

Cleo ran up, driving off the crows. The bird on the ground was an owl, its head and feathers a bloody mess. She thought it was dead, or near death, until it rushed at her with a high-pitched cry like the sound of escaping steam. She stumbled, fell, then scrambled to her feet and retreated.

The owl was smaller than she'd thought, about the size of a robin. One wing didn't fold properly. It was a young owl and wouldn't let Cleo near. No matter how slowly approached, the owl charged her with a hissing noise, and finally Cleo left to go fishing. She'd come back and try again later.

Fish and a few wild greens were almost all Cleo was eating. She hadn't touched her supplies for over a week. The moment she had put them in the ground she had begun to regard them as insurance for a rainy day. It left her feeling proud, but also hungry, at times ravenous. She craved something "good" to eat—"real food"—pancakes and sausage, scrambled eggs, a big plateful of French toast dripping with butter and maple syrup.

She drifted along the shore all the way to the

shallows at the western end of the island. The deer were there, the same three, in the water up to their bellies, feeding in the lilies. The big doe's long golden back shivered where an insect touched it. A blue jay cried a warning, and the deer raised their heads and looked right at Cleo.

"It's me, Cleo," she murmured. She wanted the majestic creatures to accept her as part of the island, not to be afraid of her. The big doe's ears twitched. She floundered up the bank, then broke for the woods, the two smaller does following closely.

Later, she found the owl hidden under a tree. She had brought a fish with her. "Here, Owl." She wriggled the fish so it looked lifelike. The owl didn't move, but didn't attack, either. At least they were looking at each other. "Here I am, Owl, and there you are. It's not so bad, is it?" She dropped the fish in the pine needles at the owl's feet.

Dragging its bad wing, the owl took the fish between its claws and swallowed it. Excited by her success, Cleo ran back to the cave and brought back two more fish. Owl ate them both.

Several times that night Cleo woke up, hoping it was morning already, she was so eager to see Owl. As soon as the light came, she was up and out. She found Owl hidden in the roots of a tree. The owl's feathers were the color of bark—it was the blue eyes that gave it away.

Each day after that, she brought Owl fish, frogs, bugs, salamanders, and grasshoppers. She was busier now than she'd ever been. Fishing and gathering took most of the day—Owl took the rest.

At first Cleo ate only wild plants that she was absolutely sure of, but little by little her "shopping list" expanded. If a plant looked good or had a good taste or smell, she'd gather some, try a bit raw, cook leaf, stem, or flower, then wait overnight to see if she lived or died. She tried the green flower spikes of cattails—the wet meadow above the cave was full of them—and found them good. They smelled a little like corn, but had a taste of their own. When she ate cattails with fish she felt as if she'd had a real meal. She tried cattail roots, too. Parts were too stringy, but other parts were like little potatoes. The roots of water lilies and arrowhead were also good.

Fish was her mainstay, but there were days when all the familiar spots yielded nothing. On one of those days, catching frogs for Owl, she knew she was ready to eat a frog herself. She caught five large frogs, severed their heads, and skinned them. With the last frog, all feeling had gone out of her. Slime and blood covered her hands. With each frog she killed, something in her had hardened. Never again would she kiss a frog.

After she ate, she fed Owl. It was always there, waiting. They became friends in a cool kind of way. If Cleo came too close Owl hissed. Its look clearly said, Keep your distance. It was healing, the bloody feathers had disappeared, and its wing didn't drag as before. Cleo was crazy about Owl's looks. "Blue Eyes, you've got such pretty feathers." Owl turned its head, peered at Cleo, blinked suavely. It was compact and neat. Its head whirled and seemed to turn in a complete circle. It was gray and brown with little tufts of fur sticking up over its ears. As Owl got stronger, it sometimes clawed its way up to a low branch where it would shut its eyes and disappear against the bark.

# Chapter *13*

Every day that Cleo survived by her own hand and skill, she felt happier. Her stomach lost its fat, her arms and legs hardened, even her fingers were tougher. Days passed without her using her hairbrush. She pulled her hair to one side, braided it, and forgot it.

Her supplies remained untouched. She had two standbys: a hot wintergreen mint tea, and a kind of everything-and-anything-in-one-pot soup. Fish heads and tails, wild onion, garlic grass, cattail pollen, milkweed pods—all went into her soup. Every day she threw in whatever her foraging turned up. One day it was blue-black mussels she dug in the shallows—tough, chewy, but protein and safe; another day it was a handful of unopened day lily pods that tasted like green beans.

Every day her soup tasted different than it had the day before—sometimes better, sometimes not, but always hot and filling.

She thought of everything as food. She found a mouse drowned in her water pail and Owl ate it. Swimming, a water snake came toward her, dark brown head raised, gently sweeping its long thick body into easy *s*'s. Usually the water snakes were shy, but this one came straight on until they were staring into one another's eyes. Cleo thought quite clearly, I can kill you and put you into my pot. As if the snake sensed her killer's thoughts, it turned and swam rapidly away.

Days passed, and nights. She was never bored. She tramped in the woods, fished, picked, and caught frogs. In the morning the sun was like a golden egg breaking through the mist. One moon-lit night she was awakened by a high mewling sound outside the cave. Thinking it was the raccoon, she charged out, yelling, and chased a fat, silver-tipped porcupine into a tree where it looked down at her with its little black dog's head. "Okay. You're all right." She went back into the cave.

Cleo dreamed of herself with Owl on her shoulder, chipmunks in her pockets—but reality was different. Al Capone ate out of her hand, but the moment she touched him he darted away. The chickadees maintained their independence, and

Owl never allowed itself to be tamed. When Cleo tried to pet it, it lay on its back, a gray fluff, clicking its beak and striking at Cleo with its claws.

In the high part of the island, Cleo found the flattened places in the grass where the deer slept. Sometimes in the morning she'd hear them in the woods, bleating in their goatlike way, and once, very early, as she was sitting in front of her fire, she became aware that she wasn't alone. Turning slowly, she saw the two young deer watching her, their heads perfect copies of each other. They remained frozen for a moment and then, on a signal Cleo never caught, disappeared into the woods.

That morning she shoved a punky log into the fire. It was still smoldering when she came back to the cave at dusk, and it smoldered all through the night. It was comforting to wake in the dark, look out of the cave, and see that dim glow. In the morning she fed the fire with leaves and twigs, added wood, and started her tea water heating. After that she kept a fire going constantly and rarely used any of her dwindling supply of matches.

As August drew to an end the days stayed clear and dry, but the nights were increasingly cold and windy. The trees faded, the grass was dry. At night the wind blew through the pines, and in the woods Owl whinnied. Mornings when she swam there was often a mist, and the water was warmer than the air. She still went everywhere barefoot, swam naked, and dressed only in a shirt and cut-offs. But at night she wore her sweat shirt.

She was aware of time passing, of the loons flying overhead, and the swiftly passing ducks, always in pairs. Were they going south? Was it time already? Time to move on? Time for her, too, then. Everything was coming to an end. Summer was nearly over. But why rush? The birds remained, and the deer, and clever Al Capone. Why leave them? Why leave Owl, and apples waiting to be gathered, and swimming in the morning, and being thin and happy? She'd have to go back sometime soon, face her father and her grandmother. There would be questions and accusations.

Of course the way she'd disappeared without a word had been wrong. They would have a right to be angry. She would apologize, take whatever punishment they had to give. But then, would they listen to her? They had never listened before. And if they did, would they understand the way she had felt when Jam died? The emptiness . . . the loneliness. . . . Could she tell them how the world had fallen apart for her, how nothing remained? The island had saved her. She would go back, but not yet.

On a hot, sultry day, Cleo was in the shallows where all kinds of lush green plants grew in abundance. The air hummed with insect sounds. Cleo hummed as she dug up a new plant, a big sturdy plant that looked like Queen Anne's lace. The leaves were coarse, hairy, unpleasant, but the root smelled sweet. That night she cooked the tubers separately, took her usual careful small bite, and set the rest aside for the next day. It tasted something like turnips, which she'd always despised, but her tastes had changed.

Fierce knifelike cramps woke her later. Hot, sweaty, her head pounding, she got out of the cave just in time to heave up everything, then leaned against a tree, spitting weakly.

All night she lay outside with her hands under her stomach, spitting weakly. When day came she was too exhausted to move. The sun came up and beat down on her.

All day she lay by the pool. It was dark when she dragged herself back into the cave and instantly fell asleep.

*Get up, Cleo.* It was her grandmother. *Oh! You smell bad.*

I'm sorry, Grandmother. I spit up. I couldn't help myself.

*You do smell. Get up this instant and wash yourself.*

Then her father was standing there, wearing his belted jacket, a smartly feathered hat, and holding a furled umbrella like a gun. *So there you are. Do you know how much trouble and time you've cost me? Time is money, and money is of the essence.*

No, Daddy, money doesn't matter. What is of the essence is living.

*Let her be,* her grandmother said imperiously. *She'll rot here.*

Please . . . what are you both doing here? I'm sick, and you're making me worse. Go away. Please? Get off my island?

*Her island,* her father said. *Listen to her.*

*Stop whining. Is that what they teach you at St. Ives? I'll have to see about that school.*

Her father lit a cigar. *I believe I have something of value on Duck Island. Summer homes, an escape from the congestion and pressures of the city—*

Oh, no! Not my island!

*Cleo?* Jam's voice was coming through a crack in the rock. Cleo heard her giggling.

Jam! Oh, Jam, where are you?

Frank Garrity was piling rocks in the entrance.

Frank, what are you doing? Will you tell Jam to come back? Will you please tell her?

Frank piled rocks, more rocks, closing her in.

Frank, is that the way they told you to control me? I want to be reasonable, but I don't think you should do this. . . .

Cleo struggled to sit up. Her heart raced. It was black all around. Jam . . . the rocks . . . her grandmother. . . . Then she saw the unblocked entrance to the cave, pale against the dark walls. It had all been a nightmare. Fever dreams.

The next day she was too weak to leave the cave. It took her several days to recover her strength, but the morning came when she was up and out, ready to swim again.

# Chapter 14

A hot day early in September.

Standing in the water, Cleo looked out over the dazzling surface of the lake. At the edge of the cove, a pair of diving loons disappeared beneath the surface, then bobbed up far from where they'd gone under. Their black heads glistened in the light.

She swam out and let herself sink down, hands clasped over her head. The water pressed around her like a velvet cloth, cutting her off from the wind, the light, and the noise of the world. Naked, she was Cleo herself, no more, no less. . . . As she surfaced she heard a faint distant clicking, like someone knocking two pebbles together, then saw a speck on the water that grew as she watched it. A motorboat. Grabbing her clothes, she retreated to the shelter of the trees.

It was Frank again, hand crooked behind him on the motor. The boat droned along the shore, past the point. The sound receded, but a moment later she heard it on the other side of the island. He was circling the island, just as he'd done the other time.

The motor cut off. What was he doing now? The crack of a twig made her heart jump. It was a still, nearly windless day. The birds seemed to have stopped their chirping. She had the feeling that the whole island, like her, was holding its breath. Staying out of sight, she moved along the shore. She heard sounds from the beach, then what she thought was the crack of an ax. She caught a whiff of gas. An oil slick lay on the water. Frank was standing by the ruins of the cabin, hands in his back pockets. He removed his orange hunting cap and ran his fingers through his bristly gray hair.

He looked intently at something on the ground. Had she left a mark, a footprint, some sign he could read? Would he find her trails and follow them to the cave?

She fought the desire to run.

"Anybody here?" he called.

He went further up the trail and called again. "I know you're up there. Come down here."

She heard him moving through the woods, calling.

Circling around him, she went back to the cave.

There she knocked down her fireplace, piled her pots and utensils inside the cave, and covered the entrance with evergreens. She looked around to see if she'd forgotten anything, then threw branches across the trails leading to the cave.

Later, concealed in the trees, she watched Frank sitting on a rock near his boat, smoking a pipe. Every so often he called. He was calling her now. "Cleo . . . I know you're there . . . Come down here!" And then in a lower voice, to himself, "Rich stupid brat."

He looked at his watch, tapped his foot, and sat there like a big self-satisfied bear. She began to think he was bluffing, didn't really know that she was here. He was just following her father's orders. *Check the island. I know you've been there once. Do it again.*

Looking up at the sky, she wished for a rainstorm so strong it would wash him off the island. Maybe a tree would fall and break his legs. Or she could set his boat adrift.

Sure, stupid. And trap him here with you. That would be perfect.

Late in the afternoon she crept up to the wet meadow and caught frogs for Owl. Its wing was healed; it could fly now, but still liked to be fed. She hooted for Owl but it didn't come.

At dusk she heard the motor and went down to

the shore. Frank was in the water up to his knees, his pants legs rolled up, fiddling with the engine. Quietly Cleo climbed a tree and watched him. The motor sputtered, then died. She thought he'd never get it going. It was almost dark when he had it idling smoothly. He climbed in, but still he didn't go. "Cleo . . . Cleo Murphy . . . Come on, Cleo. . . . Come on, honey. . . . Nobody's mad at you, but if you stay away any longer . . ."

Called her the way you called and coaxed and threatened a child.

You don't know me very well, Mr. Garrity. You don't know how I feel about the island. You don't know how I want to shout at you, but I never will because I'm not ready to leave the island yet.

The boat moved into deeper water but Cleo remained hidden until it was so far out it was nothing but a black dot again.

# Chapter 15

As Cleo settled down next to her fire, she heard Owl call, the high whinny that always sent shivers down her spine. She threw out a crayfish, and Owl, separating from the darkness, swooped down, snared the crayfish, then flew up onto a low limb to eat it.

"He's gone, Owl." Cleo stroked the owl's head. Owl clucked, then bit her finger with its curved ivory bill. "We're alone again, Owl." She was happy to be alone. Life on the island was simple and real. When she stubbed her toes she hurt, when the fish didn't bite she was hungry. Caught in the rain, she got wet. She made a fire if she was cold, and if she was tired, she slept.

Early that morning Cleo went down to the beach. The grass was flattened where he'd sat, a groove remained where his boat had been pulled up on the sand. She smoothed over the sand, picked up bits of paper.

Day after day passed. September was half over; every morning she woke up to the sun shining, the sky high and blue, the air crisp. The island turned scarlet and gold. Ducks passed overhead, and long flights of geese. The loons were gone. At dusk the geese settled in the sheltered waters around the island, coming down like a ragged mob, honking and calling.

Crouched near the shore, she often watched them, big fat black-and-white Canadian geese. Whole squadrons landed in the water, and other flights roared straight up. At night she heard them grumbling on the lake.

She gathered apples, grapes, different sweet berries, and acorns, which she boiled and then roasted over the fire. There was enough of everything. Her stores remained untouched, a source of pride.

She didn't swim as she had before. The air was chilly, the water too cold. She dipped in and out, then dressed quickly.

At night she sat with her back to the cave wall, the fire heating her face. Owl was usually there clucking like a hen to be fed and petted. The insects were gone and sometimes she slept out, looking up into the night sky, into that stillness and those countless quivering stars. In the morning there would be a cold mist over the lake—once there was even a light frost. Cleo lay snug in her sleeping bag, watching her breath, waiting for the sun to warm the air. Soon it would be time to leave. . . . Soon. . . . Soon. . . .

For a week the days were summery, the nights cold and crisp. She sunbathed on the rocks, slept, was suddenly lazier than she had been for months. The sun beat on her head. She felt the currents of the wind, the trees swaying, saw clouds passing in great processions and the lake flowing in every direction. The whole island throbbed.

Unseen forces streamed through her . . . the island flowing through her . . . herself flowing through the island. She was filled with joy past comprehension. *I am the island . . . the island is me. . . .*

One afternoon the weather changed abruptly. All day, the sun had been like liquid gold. Then a belt of gray clouds appeared on the horizon, and a strange stillness hung over the lake. She was far from the cave, down by the shallows watching the deer. One of the smaller deer had hurt its leg. It was slower than the others. She felt the storm coming, but lingered until the first crack of thunder sent the deer running for shelter.

Leaves and birds were swept up in the wind.

Trees bent. Cleo scrambled onto the rocks. Exhilarated, she felt the power of the wind, felt her own power. Her shirt flattened against her body. She leaned against the gusting air. Thunder growled, rain spattered the land, and the sky darkened. Only when lightning struck did she return to the cave.

It was a violent storm. The driving, drenching rain lasted through the night and in the morning everything was damp—clothing, sleeping bag, the wood she kept stacked inside the cave. She couldn't start a fire. The wind continued to blow, and the sky was covered with gray scudding clouds. The trees were stripped almost bare, and for the first time she had an unobstructed view of the lake through the trees. Many trees had fallen. The island, which had been so green and lush, full of birds and insects, activity and sound, was like an empty house whose tenants had fled. It was a sign for her. Now it *was* time to leave.

She decided to go immediately, as soon as the lake settled down. She spent the morning gathering her things. Every possession was important—sleeping bag, knapsacks, ax and shovel, her pail and pots, even her mason jar, which had somehow survived everything.

The canoe would have to be tipped over and emptied before she could start for Dundee. "Dundee," she said. It sounded unreal, but before the day was past she would be there. And from there, home. She would see her father and her grand-mother.

Several times she called Owl. By late afternoon the lake was calm. She broke down her fireplace and piled rocks in the entrance to the cave. Some-day she would come back. She made a last effort to find Owl, then with the knapsack on her back, she went quickly down through the trees.

She had "dressed up"—put on her overalls and boots, combed her hair, even tried to see her face in the pool. Soon she would be looking at people again, and they would be looking at her, at the surface self that seemed to matter so much in the world.

At the stream she looked for the overhanging tree where she always tied up the canoe. The tree was down—the storm's work. It lay sprawled across the water, a mass of broken limbs. At first she thought the canoe had broken loose and drifted away. Then she saw it, caught underneath the tree.

She jumped into the stream and tried to pull the canoe free, yanking and tugging it from every side. The tree had fallen on top of it, crushed it. Even after she knew she no longer had a canoe, she kept trying to free it.

# Chapter 16

Cleo stared at the smashed canoe. She would never get off the island now. For a moment her mind blurred; she couldn't think of anything except that winter was coming and she would die. She ran toward the highest point of the island, vainly hoping to see her rescue coming over the water. The lake, as always, was empty. She faced the mainland. Dundee was there, in that direction. She tried to calm herself by following a gull dipping and rising, soaring toward the distant shore. How easy it was for a bird.

"If only . . . if only . . ." she repeated, and at the same moment realized how stupidly she was acting. She could swim, couldn't she? What was it— five miles to Dundee? Farther than she'd ever swum, but she was strong now. Could she really do it . . . swim to Dundee? She could do it. Then and there she kicked off her boots, left them on shore, tied her overalls and sweater into a bundle around her neck, and entered the water.

It was numbingly cold. She set a strong steady pace that took her quickly away from the island. Pausing to rest, she saw the island stretched out behind her, but ahead only the choppy surface of the lake. She struck out again.

When she looked back again, the island was smaller, but still visible. It was going to be a long swim. She couldn't keep up her initial vigorous pace. Doubts entered her mind. Could she do it? Swim . . . then rest. . . . The waves seemed to push her back. For a while she floated on her back, then swam hard again. Her clothing dragged behind her.

The wind picked up. A wave sloshed over her. She swallowed water, choked, coughed. She was alone in the middle of the lake. How much farther? She was tired. Had she swum a mile? Swim . . . rest . . . swim. . . . You can do it. On and on like a robot. *Do it.* Push weariness and fear aside. Hadn't she done everything that way? Come to the island . . . found the cave . . . learned to live by herself . . .

Waves broke in her face. She swam a few strokes, lost her rhythm, stopped, had to rest. She thought about sinking down, resting at the bottom of the lake.

A duck flew over. Tears came to her eyes. It was too far. How far had she swum? A mile? Two miles? She wasn't strong enough.

She turned back, the wind behind her now. Hard to raise her arms . . . The island so far away. So tired. . . . Her arms fell into the water. Couldn't. Had to. Keep going. Go . . . go . . . go . . .

Blind, dumb momentum drove her on. Arms and legs turning to stone . . .

She hit something, grabbed, clung. Eyes closed. What was it? A floating branch? A log? Rocks? She was disoriented, felt nothing, saw nothing. She had been swimming so long, her mind lost in dreams.

She had struck a rock, the pile of rocks that lay off the tip of the island. The island, so close she didn't believe it. The shore was not a hundred feet away.

She held to the rock a long time before she found the strength to swim the rest of the way to shore. On the island she stumbled up to the cave, where she burrowed into the evergreens and instantly fell into a deep dreamless sleep. When she woke it was light. Her teeth chattered. She went down to the stream, retrieved her knapsack and her boots at the shore, and came back to the cave. She huddled, chilled to her bones. The day was bright and sunny, a smell of dried leaves in the air. She built a fire, made strong mint tea and went back to bed. Another day passed before she felt like getting out.

The island was pale, bare, and open. The lake glittered. She sat for a long time looking toward the mainland so distinct but now so impossibly far. The lake was too cold—there was no time to condition for another try. She could never swim to the mainland now.

Around noon a plane passed overhead. She heard the distant drone, then saw the chalk-thin jet trail. Was anyone up there looking down? Ridiculous to think she could be seen. Still, she hoped—she had no right to hope, but she couldn't help dreaming about being rescued. Frank would come to the island again, or her father. Or maybe Glenn, who'd outfitted her. She *had* signed her name to the sales slip. Maybe he'd seen something in the newspapers about her being missing. He'd gotten in touch with her family and they figured out where she was. He would come looking for her. This time she wouldn't hide, just take her stuff and hop into his motorboat.

She woke to where she was, sitting on a rock, looking down at her bare feet, doing nothing to help herself.

She rebuilt her fireplace, hung up her pots, and later roped her yellow shirt to the oak tree on top of the island. When the wind blew, the shirt filled out like a flag. Nearby she built a fire on top of a rock. The wind blew and the fire blazed up too fast and high. Sparks leaped. She let the fire die out, but piled up brush and wood. If a low-flying plane came over, she'd start the fire quickly.

No planes went by low enough to see her distress flag, or for her to start a fire. Days passed. No boats appeared on the water. It was hard to keep hope alive. Owl didn't return, though other animals were still active. She saw signs of the beaver and the porcupine, the raccoon continued to paw through her ashes, and almost every day she saw the deer. Now their gaze seemed to say, "What? You're still here?"

In the smashed canoe she found the paddle intact, held it, her hands gripping it in the accustomed way. She even stroked the air a couple of times.

You're all ready. But where's your boat, dummy?

"I might just decide to build a boat." She stroked the air decisively. Well, maybe not a boat, but a raft. Anyone could build a raft. She'd paddle it across the lake and not even get her feet wet. She could do things—knew it—why not a raft? The more she thought, the less fantastic it seemed. She was so quick to jump into things. Would she do this the way she'd jumped into the lake? No, this time she'd think things through.

In the bays and in the shallows where the wind blew in from the lake, tangles of trees and logs had drifted up on shore. She balanced on a log. It sank slightly, but held her. What she needed were several of these big logs, and some way of holding them together. Rope would do it, more rope than she had. She thought of grape vines—the trees were loaded with grapes—but when she tested the vines they snapped. Another day passed. Another day wasted. Then she thought of the cabin, and spent half a day picking through the ashes, salvaging enough bent nails to fill her mason jar. She brought back a number of charred boards as well, to nail across the logs. In her mind the raft was built already.

It turned out to be slow, cold work. The logs were either too heavy for her to move, or waterlogged, or caught under the tangle of trees. All day she was in and out of the icy water, and kept a fire going on the beach.

Slow work chopping branches, pulling, prying—hard, mulish work. It took her two days just to maneuver the first log up on the shore. It took even longer to free a second log. One more would do it.

One morning she woke to find a snake in her sleeping bag, grabbed it, and crushed it with a stone. The body was still writhing when she cut off the head. She cooked it, ate it, then went to work.

As she worked the rain came, a downpour that sent her racing for the cave. She slept through the morning, got a fire going under a rock, made tea, and slept again—slept away the hours. A week of hauling logs had worn her out.

The next day she was back at work and had the third log freed by noontime and lined up with the other two. Using the ax as a hammer, she nailed a board across each end, then nailed the rest of the salvaged boards in between.

The raft barely moved when she tried to push it into the water. She cut a long pole and pried one corner, then the other, inching the raft forward. Corner to corner. The pole slipped. She skinned her knee, and blood flowed. Bit by bit the raft slid into the water until it was afloat.

She had to try it out at once. It was long and narrow like a canoe, but not nearly as maneuverable. She knelt to work the paddle, keeping the raft close to shore. The wind blew the raft gently along the shore. It was beautiful, and Cleo enjoyed the ride. She passed the inlet, the high land, approached the beach. The wind picked up as the raft slid down the length of the island.

The raft creaked, waves broke across Cleo's legs. One of the boards popped loose, then another. Cleo tried to guide the raft into shore, but couldn't get it to turn. It swept past the beach. In a moment it would reach the end of the island, and the rocks. She saw the rocks. Too late. The raft was moving too fast, the logs were separating. She thrust the paddle into the water, but couldn't stop the forward motion of the raft. At the last moment she jumped off and watched helplessly as the raft crashed into the rocks, tilted up, and split apart.

# Chapter 17

All along Cleo had thought she still might leave in style. But now the island and the lake and the wind had humbled her. As she climbed wearily out of the water she could hear them whispering and giggling over her. Cleo, you fool, the wind cried, and the island chuckled silently, and the lake gurgled in agreement. Cleo, you fool . . . you fool . . . you fool . . .

She had spent days making the raft, had eaten all her food. There were no more boards, no more nails. Could she cross the lake astride a single log? There was no time left now for trials and experiments and hoping she could make a raft, hoping she could sail it, hoping someone would come and save her. Hoping, hoping, hoping. . . . Winter was approaching and she was without food, or real shelter, or warm clothes.

"What do I do now?" she cried out. Then she listened, as if someone would answer. She heard the wind and the water—nothing else. The island didn't care. It wouldn't cheer if she struggled. It wouldn't cry if she lost. The island was indifferent to her tears and cries. It had always been indifferent to her, to her self-pity and self-loathing, to the masks and disguises she hid behind; indifferent, too, to her conceit that she was herself at last, one with nature. All vanity, foolishness, stupidity. She was alone, isolated and forgotten, with no expectations except the one nature forced on her. You're going to die. Say it.

"I'm going to die." She could barely hear herself. "Louder!" The minute she stopped saying it she started dreaming of rescuers again.

It was meaningless. Did she think she could live just because she wanted to? Jam had wanted to live, and so had her mother.

"You're going to die. You're going to die. Die. Die. Die."

The sun shone, the light was beautiful, the trees and rocks glittered, the whole world gleamed. There was that good smell of dry crisp leaves in the air. How could she die? How could anything die surrounded by all this beauty? But there was death everywhere. Big fish ate small fish, crows ate robins, and robins ate caterpillars and worms. In the woods the trees struggled for light.

It was October. The trees were almost completely bare. The nights were cold, getting colder. Already there was frost on the ground. She thought of the winter coming, the snow, the storms, the cold. The lake would freeze and she could walk on it. Yes, she could cross the lake on foot. How long would it be? Ten weeks? Twelve? Three months? Would she live till then?

She imagined her death. One day she'd be too weak to get out of the sleeping bag. The fire would go out and she'd slowly freeze to death. She saw herself, hair grown long as grass, stretched out flat, disappearing into the ground. When spring came what was left of her would bloat and stink like the dead fish washed up on shore. The raccoon would sniff out her body, dig his sharp nose into her eyes and gnaw her soft brains.

She sank down. She was going to die. But something in her didn't believe it, would never believe it. Hope, pushed down, kept bouncing back.

Three months till the lake froze. She'd need a fire day and night, stacks and stacks of wood. Plenty of wood around, but where would she keep it out of the weather? The cave was too small for her and all the wood she'd need. Besides, wind came through the opening, rain splashed in. . . .

And what about food? Her mind jumped from

one thing to another. What was there to eat in winter? And clothes? She had only a sweat shirt, no hat, gloves, warm pants, or socks.

She saw herself huddled by an open fire, the wind blowing. What good would the fire be if all the heat blew away? If she didn't starve, she'd freeze to death. Fire . . . shelter . . . food . . . clothes. . . . She looked out over the empty waters, saw the distant line of the mainland. So close . . . so impossibly far. . . . When the lake froze she'd cross over in a day—less than a day. She saw herself crossing the ice, running, nothing would stop her. Why did she have to die when she wanted so much to live?

She'd be like the old oak. It lived on rock, the wind battered it, storms split its limbs, but it lived. It didn't give up. It lived. Maybe nature would let her live, too, if she didn't give up . . . if she tried, and was clever, and strong—and lucky as well.

# Chapter 18

The day after the raft was destroyed Cleo set to work again and started building a windbreak around the fireplace. In the back of her mind she had an idea that if she could build the wall right to the cave, she could make a room, but she couldn't really think about that yet.

Early each morning, when she had the most strength, she gathered rocks and piled them on both sides of the fireplace. Nothing careful or precise, heaviest rocks on the bottom, smaller rocks on top. It was hard work. At first it didn't look like anything, just a pile of rock and rubble. Everything had to be done quickly. Every day it grew colder. Build the windbreak, gather food, stack up wood. Time was her enemy. So much time wasted already. She was impatient, bashed her fingers on the rocks.

For days all she thought about were rocks, lugging rocks, rolling rocks end over end, straining to lift rocks into place. At the end of each day her back ached, and she slept as if she'd been clubbed.

It was more than a week, maybe ten days—she didn't think about time too carefully—and she had built a sturdy, waist-high wall behind the fireplace. Enough, she thought. That night she slept by the fire. Above, the icy stars. Wind buffeted the trees. Wrapped in her sleeping bag, half sheltered from the wind, she dreamed of rocks.

The next day she went back to work on the wall, piling rock, moving the wall on either side of the fireplace toward the cave. When she couldn't stand the sight of another rock she went gathering or fishing, but not for long. She wasn't eating much —one real meal a day—only enough to sustain her.

It rained. A gray, dirty-white sky. The color had gone out of everything but the evergreens. The days were getting shorter. There was never enough daylight for everything she had to do. At night she worked by a firebrand set into the ground. She worked tired, worked exhausted, didn't dare stop. She became rough, dirty, hard and scrawny. If she had a minute she threw some roots and greens into a pot for a broth that she sipped when she took a break from work. She kept the fire going, didn't dare be careless about that.

She was aware of time passing—too aware of how little progress she'd made. Winter was coming—coming in on her. The stone walls reached the cave, were highest against the cave, but not as high as she wanted. The higher she went, the harder the work became. She began thinking how to pitch a roof across the top, bridge the walls, close in that space. It would give her two rooms—the cave and a stone room where she could store wood and keep a fire going under shelter, even in the worst weather.

She hadn't started storing food, didn't know what she was going to do about clothes.

Wear her overalls over her jeans and stay warm in front of the fire—but without food, what good would her fire and stone walls be?

One day a rock she was lifting slipped and hit her foot and she hopped around for the rest of the day. That night she nursed her foot before the fire and worried about food. How long would the fish continue to bite? What would she do when they stopped biting? Maybe she could dry them on the rocks in the sun. The next morning she went fishing and took three bass. She sliced thin fillets, put them on the rocks to dry, and threw heads, tails, and bones into her soup. At night she continued drying the fish on makeshift racks between the fire and the stone wall. Worried about the raccoon, she woke at every sound. A roof would keep the raccoon out.

Every chance she got she caught and dried fish, storing them in rough bags that she fashioned from long cattail leaves. She dried other things, too—roots of waterplants, grapes, apples, and acorns. She had a bag almost full of dry fish, another with roots, and her big knapsack stuffed with apples and grapes. The acorns she stored in the supply pit. Her food supplies were building up, but it was never enough. No way of knowing how much she'd need when the snow fell.

One day returning to the cave, she saw the raccoon sitting on the stone wall with something in his paws. She yelled, went for him with the shovel. He raced for the woods, Cleo after him, but he disappeared. She went back to the cave. The raccoon had found the dried fish, eaten it all. She went after him again, to the pine where she knew he slept, and banged on the tree with the shovel. His face appeared in a notch above her, an innocent teddy bear look.

"You ate my fish," she screamed. "I'll kill you." She'd eat him the way he'd eaten what was hers. Eat his flesh and wear his skin. The thought filled her with satisfaction. At first she was mad, vengeful, then she began to think of it seriously. She ate fish and frogs, why not the raccoon? And the beaver, the muskrat, whatever she could catch. She knew the hollow log where the porcupine slept. And the deer? she asked herself. She didn't know if she could kill a deer. They were so big, so beautiful and swift. But a deer would feed and clothe her till the ice froze.

She sharpened a long pole for a spear, and carried it everywhere along with her knapsack, knife, and shovel. Catching frogs and fish had been her first lessons in killing. Was she hard enough for a raccoon or muskrat? Her face twisted at the thought of the kill, but her hand would be steady.

She stalked a muskrat in the shallows. The snakes and frogs were gone, the ducks out of reach. The muskrat slipped through the water, looking nervously back at her, sensing her purpose. Inching her way along the bank, she jabbed at the muskrat, missed, and fell into the water.

The beaver didn't let her near. She heard the wet flap of geese overhead and followed their flight and looked hungrily at the chickadees she had taught to feed from her hand. Such tiny birds, but she had to kill something, prove that she could. She sat with a handful of seeds. A black and white chickadee tumbled down from a tree, a tiny stuffed clown. A quick hop and it was in her hand, pecking at seed. She grabbed for it. Too late. She was sorry, and then she was glad, and then she was sorry again.

Just by chance, she killed a porcupine. As she walked in the woods with her spear, a porcupine shuffled past. She broke into a run, caught up with him easily. He climbed a tree; she poked him down with the spear, didn't think, just acted. He turned on her, quills raised, lashed out with his tail. She jumped aside, drove the spear into his body. Blood spurted . . . thick red blood. It made her crazy. She drove the spear in again . . . again . . . again . . . The porcupine lay still.

Her heart pumped with excitement and shock. There was dirt in the porcupine's paws. The quills were black and silver. He smelled of blood and pine needles.

She cut off his head, tied a rope around his forelegs, and dragged him back to the cave, where she slit the carcass from neck to belly, cleaned out the entrails, and wiped the cavity with grass. The body was still warm.

With the sharp point of the knife she separated skin from flesh, cutting, tearing, pulling. Needle-like quills caught in her hands. She ripped and pulled, grunting at the work.

It was done. The pink carcass lay on the ground, a piece of meat. She threw one of the legs into the fire. The meat tasted like wood, but she chewed it to the bone. She thought of the porcupine's little dog face. She wasn't sorry. Chance had brought the porcupine across her path. His bad luck, her good luck. If he hadn't been at that spot at that moment, he might have lived his life out. Why did some die and others live? Was it all chance? Why had her mother died? Why Jam? There was something hard and inexplicable in the world that couldn't be understood, that she would never understand. She had never wanted to kill an animal. But she had. And she would do it again.

# Chapter *19*

A balefully bright winter light swept across the island. Snow was coming. A belt of gray clouds girdled the horizon. It snowed, a fine, spitting snow, damp and cold, and then it rained. The gray gloomy days put Cleo into a frenzy of activity. The floor of the roofless stone room was sodden. She planned a roof—solid poles, one next to the other, to be covered with bark, leaves, and dirt.

Holding the ax with both hands, she hacked away at the base of a young, straight tree with such fervor the tree fell before she realized she'd chopped through. It happened so fast she couldn't get out from under, and fell down, the tree on top of her. It took a moment to realize she wasn't hurt. She flattened herself, crawled out from under, took up the hatchet again, lopped off the top, and began trimming branches.

She no longer expected anything to happen the way she planned. Things happened the way they happened. Nothing was easy, but that didn't matter, either, not as long as she kept working. One thing, and then the next.

She dragged the pole back to the cave, lifted one end to the top of the stone wall, then raised the other end to the opposite wall. That day she cut two more poles and set them in place. Lying in her bag that night, her head in the opening of the cave, she looked up at the sky through the three poles.

The next day she cut and trimmed three more poles and set them in place. After a few more days' work she began covering the poles. Bark was good, but it was difficult to get enough good pieces. What worked best were layers of overlapped evergreen boughs that she cut in the woods and carried back stacked on her head.

For an entrance just big enough for her to crawl in and out, she pulled some stones free on the low side of one wall near the fireplace. She covered the floor with pine needles, later on found a flat rock to tip across the opening to keep out animals. No place to stand up inside the stone room. Even on the high side near the cave she had to stoop over.

The first time it rained, she crawled in and out rearranging the roof coverings, adding boughs, but no matter what she did, it never stopped leaking completely, or in unexpected places. She stuffed moss and mud between the chinks in the stone. It smelled piney inside, and at night, with the fire burning and smoke drifting up through the roof, the room was filled with a warm yellow light.

She stacked wood inside, more wood all around the outside. From a distance her shelter looked like a pile of stone and wood, a low bushy mound with a green top.

It was cold all through November. Rain and snow. She counted and recounted her remaining matches, kept the fire alive constantly. Despite everything she never caught cold, and endured things now she never would have thought possible. She enjoyed testing herself—walking in the snow barefoot, not eating for two or three days at a time. She was making herself strong for the bitter cold time to come. She made rules for herself— no eating until she had stored some food, catch and dry two fish before eating one.

As the nights got colder she slept closer to the fire. Most nights the smoke drifted up through the roof, but when the wind howled across the island the smoke blew back. Then her eyes smarted and her throat got sore. Several times she was driven out into the frigid air until the smoke cleared.

She hauled stones again to build a chimney. She placed a large flat stone over the fireplace and left an opening in back, around which she arranged stones, then daubed them with mud and sticks. More stones, then more mud. The chimney grew, a crooked, free-standing column, that finally poked up through the roof.

When she built the fire, she half expected the chimney to collapse. Smoke went up the chimney. Crouching, she built the fire higher. It was gold at its heart, and as she looked into its shadows and lights she saw figures moving around, animal figures—elk and bears and fox. They were dancing in the great hall of a castle. She saw herself with a crown on her head. Her arms were bare. She was brave and strong. Around her in the shadows the animals danced.

That night it turned bitter cold. Cleo slept with all her clothes, huddled close to the fire, woke once, threw on wood, then lay there looking at the light flickering.

There was a hard frost on the ground the next morning. All day flights of geese passed overhead in long crooked lines pointing south. Each time Cleo saw them she watched, waiting for them to descend. Every afternoon the geese dropped down into the protected waters of the island, honking and calling back and forth. They were enormous, well fed. Cleo crouched at the water's edge. At her least movement the geese rose nervously.

She waited, cold and stiff, her hands and feet

numb. Several geese came out of the water. Fat round birds with white breasts and long black heads. One waddled toward her, neck extended like a black snake. Suddenly Cleo flung her arms around the goose. The bird honked wildly, battered her with its wings. They crashed into the bushes. The air was full of feathers. The other geese rose with a roar of wings and water. The goose bit Cleo's arm. She grabbed for the neck, and in the scuffle dropped her knife. The goose broke free, half flying, lurching toward the water. She grabbed at its leg, the bird, wet, slippery, slipping away. She couldn't hold it, and it rose into the air, beating at her with its wings.

The goose came down some distance away, out of reach, and lay with its head flat on the water. On her hands and knees, Cleo watched the bird drift away.

A few nights later she heard the raccoon again, sniffling outside the wall. What did he want? She had nothing for him. Some roots, a few pieces of dried fish. She yelled, and he was quiet for a moment, then she heard him rustling over her head. Hunched over, knife in her fist, she waited, then stabbed up through the roof several times in rapid succession. She listened. He was gone.

Cold day followed cold day. Winter was here. A crust of ice covered the island. The moon at night lit the icy limbs of trees, turned them to glass. The island glittered. Fragile fingers of ice crept out along the protected bays.

The fishing was poor. In the woods, Cleo's steps crackled on stiff dead leaves. Everywhere she came across deer tracks, saw the deer browsing in the trees. They were smooth as gold—the two younger deer grown nearly as big as the mother, but one still limped.

At night Cleo sat in the dimness of the stone room, drinking tea, and thought about killing the deer. She'd killed the porcupine, failed with the goose. The deer were enormous. Even if she got close enough, how could she do it? Killing the raccoon made better sense.

Hunger never left her, and the fear of the hunger to come. Small red worms, as well as grubs she found under the bark of trees, went into her stew pot. The soft inner bark of trees tasted good, too, and bits of it went into her pot. Sometimes the stew was not much more than warm, slightly flavored water.

At night the moment she heard the raccoon she grabbed the knife and ducked out, but he always disappeared before she could reach him.

One day, at dusk, crouching in front of the fire, stirring her stew pot, she heard the raccoon outside again. The rock was rolled away from the entrance, but instead of rushing out after him she picked up a chunk of wood, eased back into the cave, and waited. Soon he came boldly to the entrance, paused for a moment, outlined against the light, then stepped into the room. Her grip tightened around the chunk of wood. The fire flared and she saw the raccoon on his hind legs next to the pot.

Bent over, Cleo charged, driving the raccoon toward the back of the room. Now she was between him and the opening. The raccoon froze, down on all fours, humped up as big as a dog. She lunged, swung the wood. He went swiftly up the wall, burrowing through the roof. She knocked him loose. With a hiss he came at her, teeth bared. She brought the wood down on his back. Something cracked. She hit him again. He lay still. Panting, she poked him, then turned him over on his back. He was dead.

# Chapter 20

Crouched in the stiff, brittle grass Cleo observed the deer. She was hungry and cold. She was always hungry and cold. Hungryandcold—one word, one sound that rarely left her. Hungryandcold . . . hungryandcold . . .

She concentrated on the big doe, the long supple neck, the large ears smooth and delicate as china, the unswerving gaze of those luminous eyes. She wanted the big doe. She dreamed about chunks of meat simmering in the pot. The last of the raccoon's meat was gone, the carcass boiled till every scrap of meat was cleaned from the bones. For several days now only the bones remained.

She lay there watching the deer, imagining it all, the way she would catch the big doe by surprise, the moment when she'd rise up and plunge in the knife. Her only fear was that she would be too stiff, too slow, and the deer would escape.

The deer's breath rose as they browsed in the snow. Cleo blew softly on her fingers, rewrapped the rags around her hands, then pulled down the sleeves of her sweat shirt. She could never get her hands warm enough. Her knuckles were cracked, and her hands and feet ached all the time. Her head was warm, though, thanks to the raccoon. She had stretched and pegged the pelt on the ground, and scraped it clean. When it dried, she had made a fur shawl, which she pulled over her head and pinned beneath her chin with a clasp made from a raccoon foot. Even in the coldest wind her head was always warm.

For days now she had been observing the deer, following their paths down to the shallows, where they were still able to dig plants in the wet places. In the evening they followed other paths to high sheltered places where they slept. How close could she come? She needed to come closer, very close. She crept forward. Their heads came up. They turned, looked at her, then moved off, the big doe in front, the one with the bad leg last.

The wind came up later and snow started to fall, big flakes that stung her cheeks. She returned to the shelter, brought in armfuls of wood, built up the fire. She cracked the remains of the raccoon's bones, sucked the marrow, then cooked them again with a few roots, some bark, and a sliver of the remaining dried fish.

She had stopped fishing. A skin of ice, too thin to support her, ringed the island. Every bit of food that remained she doled out sparingly. Her world had shrunk. She felt shrunken herself . . . scratchy, narrow, tight and bony. She no longer menstruated. Her hair hung in a long, wild tangle. She sat close to the fire, and drank hot broth that scarcely satisfied her. The big doe was smart and wary, and knew Cleo was an enemy. How would she get close enough to kill?

She dozed off, thinking, If it's snowing when I wake up, I'll die . . . if not, I'll live. When she woke it was still snowing.

*That's right, you're going to die.* The voice seemed to come from the dark corners of the room. *No more Cleo. So sad.*

The voice didn't surprise her. She sang and talked aloud to herself constantly. To hear another voice seemed good.

"No, I'm not going to die," she said. "I have to get closer to the deer. I could make a bow and arrow, shoot them from a distance . . ."

A laugh from the corner. *How are you going to do that?*

"I could," Cleo said, "but it would take too long.

I'll dig a hole on one of the deer trails. When they fall in—"

*Dig a hole in the frozen ground? Smart.*

"Shut up! I'm sick of talking to you. Another thing I could do is pull down the top of a sapling, make a snare, and—"

*You're the sapling.*

"—pull down the sapling," Cleo said in a loud voice, "tie a rope to the end, and when the deer pass over, they'll step in and then—"

*Step into my parlor said the dope to the deer.*

Cleo grabbed a chunk of firewood and hurled it into the dark corner.

Early the next morning at dawn she was perched in a tree over one of the deer paths. The sky was white behind the evergreens, the snow had stopped. On the ground, the snow had drifted into dips and crevices. She hadn't eaten anything that morning; it was hard to stay alert. She fell into a dream of the big doe passing beneath her. She would fall on her . . . cling to her neck . . . drive the knife into her heart.

She woke with a start. The deer were directly beneath her. She willed herself to move, to fall on the big doe, but her legs and arms, cold and stiff, wouldn't obey. The deer moved on.

Later that same day she watched them feeding

among the apple trees. The wind blew toward her, muffling her sounds. She slid slowly along the ground, moving closer, so close she could see the play of muscle under their skin. Knife in her fist, she rested for a moment. The deer chewed noisily. She inched forward slowly, slowly, close now, closer than she'd ever been. The deer breathed and snuffled. Only one chance. If she missed the first strike the deer would escape. Close now, as close as she dared be, waiting for the big doe to turn her head away.

*Now.* Cleo's skin shivered, tightened. *Now.* She rose. The big doe's head turned—those large startled eyes. Cleo moved—only a step separated her and the big doe—she flung herself forward. The doe was already flying, all four feet in the air, sailing through the trees.

Cleo went slowly back to the cave, fighting the panicky thoughts that grabbed at her. The sky was darkening. It was getting colder. A bank of storm clouds were spread across the horizon. She felt snow in the air and brought extra wood into the stone room, stacking it on both sides of the fireplace. Her movements were slow and stiff, and she hit her head several times entering and leaving.

That night as she slept she was aware of the wind shifting and the snow falling.

In the morning she stepped into the glare of

snow. A thick heavy blanket of white lay across the island. Everything was white and still, every branch and twig loaded with snow. She took a few steps and sank down. She followed the deer's fresh tracks down to the inlet, then stood at a distance watching them pawing under the snow for moss and lichens. When the deer moved on, she gathered the same moss and lichen for her pot.

They were doubly wary with her now. The least whiff of her and they moved away. They nibbled the apple twigs, pawed in the snow for apples. The few apples that remained on the tree were out of reach.

In the cave Cleo experimented with a length of rope, making a lariat with a slip knot. Once on TV she had seen a snare made to capture an eagle. This one would capture a deer.

Near the apple trees, she spread the lariat in the snow, then pulled the top of a sapling down and tied the free end of the rope to it. She pinned the top of the tree to the ground with a forked stick. When a deer caught its foot in the lariat, the forked stick would be jarred free, and the sapling would spring up, tightening the rope around the animal's foot.

She checked the snare twice that day, watching as the deer returned to paw through the snow for apples. The snare remained untouched. Later she climbed an apple tree and picked twigs and apples that were beyond the deer's reach. Small, mealy brown fruits. She ate some herself but left the best ones in the snare.

The next day, hidden and watching, she saw the deer, their ears twitching nervously, move gingerly around the snare. That night she dreamed about the deer, the way they would lie in their deep snow holes, waiting for her to come.

She gathered more apple twigs and spread them thickly all around the snare, careful not to dislodge the forked stick. A pale, nearly colorless sun showed through the tangle of trees. The deer came late in the afternoon, single file, casting long shadows across the snow, the big doe in front, the lame one last. Where Cleo had spread the twigs across the trap, the big doe stopped, sniffed, turned aside. The second deer followed, but the one with the bad leg hesitated, sniffed, then began browsing. It found one of the apples and searched for more.

The deer was standing directly over the snare. Cleo leaned forward. The sapling whipped into the air. The deer recoiled, one of its hind legs caught by the rope. Cleo darted forward. The deer leaped up. A hoof caught Cleo in the shoulder as she drove the knife into its body. The animal cried out. She drove the knife in again. The deer grunted, sighed quietly, died. Cleo looked around. She was acutely aware of every single thing, of the silence, of her aloneness. The two other deer had disappeared. She shuddered. A black smear spread across the velvet fur. Nearby, a woodpecker hammered at a rotten apple limb.

# Chapter 21

The storms came, one after another, a week of storms, blowing snow and ferocious winds that kept Cleo close to her shelter. For three days she hardly went out. All that could be seen outside the stone room was the crooked chimney sticking up through the snow.

She tunneled out to chop wood and dip water from the pool. The snow-spattered deer carcass stood against a tree. She had cut away most of the useful venison. Days were short, and she spent a good part of them chopping and hauling wood. Three logs a day kept the fire smoldering constantly.

She raised the ax above her head. It whistled through the air, cracked into the wood. The sound echoed across the island. Left, right, yellow chips flying. Blood rushed to her cheeks. She grunted with each stroke. Three . . . four . . . five . . . ten strokes and she was halfway through a heavy limb. Another ten strokes and she had her first log for the fire. She tied a rope around it, dragged it back.

It felt good to be out, to stretch and move. She heard the raucous voices of the crows near the deer carcass. She shouted, and the crows flew off. It was a still day, a good day for a signal fire. She tied snowshoes to her boots. She had made them from forked branches that she'd crisscrossed with strips of deer hide. Crude, but they got her over the deep snow.

Holding a smoldering brand from the fire she climbed to the top of the island where she started a smoky brush fire. Maybe someone would see it. Around her she saw the deer's trails, the holes they cleared in the snow to rest and watch, facing the wind. She followed their trails now, not for food, but the way she would follow a friend. She needed something living, a creature like herself, someone she could look at and talk to. She heard them ahead of her, snorting, but when she got there they were gone.

Going back to the cave she gathered seeds from dried tufts of grass sticking up through the snow. She still fed the birds. It was wonderful when she felt the chickadees' nearly weightless bodies on her palm, saw them take seed from her.

When she could, she tried the ice on the lake. The ice had moved out, but the open waters were still unfrozen. In places she could see water beneath the ice and bubbles of air. She carried a heavy stone and dropped it ahead on the new ice. If it held, she went further, and tried the stone again until it went through. Then she turned back.

When the ice was thick enough she chopped out a hole with the side of her shovel and fished, standing on a piece of bark to keep her feet from freezing. Even in the protected bays she could stay only a little while before the wind drove her in. She caught fish, not a lot, but they added variety to her diet. Each day she ate her one meal at noon—a strip of blackened venison, roots, and a handful of seeds in a pot of boiling water. She sipped the broth slowly, saving the meat for last. Sometimes when the storms raged and she was kept in for long periods, she thought of where she was, hidden away. If she died, she could remain here for eternity, forgotten. Her body would decay and sink back into the earth. But what of her inner self, her voice, the part of her that seemed to live apart from her body? Would that self also disappear? Would nothing remain?

She thought of Jam and knew there must be a

spirit in the world, because Jam's spirit and her mother's spirit were with her all the time. Those who mattered, those you loved, stayed with you forever. Had she loved enough? She thought of her grandmother and her father, and felt remorse.

Sometimes at the end of a day, tired and aware of how alone she was, she thought despairingly that the lake would never freeze. Then she sang so loudly and enthusiastically that her throat was sore afterward.

She kept busy. Even when she was forced indoors by the weather, she had things to do. Kneeling in the yellow light of the fire, she cut the deerskin into a crude pair of leggings, then with a nail drilled holes in the deerskin and tied the pieces together with long strips of leather.

Besides the leggings, she was also working on a pair of mittens. Slow work. The light was poor, her tools primitive, but she was glad to keep busy. Waiting for the lake to freeze, she felt herself standing at the very edge of loneliness, between the island and the world. There were times when she ached for a human voice. Often she thought about Owl and wondered where it had gone.

One day the deer were gone. She hadn't seen them for several days—no sign of them anywhere, no fresh tracks or cleared places in the snow. The old tracks were filling with snow. The deer were nowhere on the island. They must have crossed the ice to the mainland. She went immediately out on the ice to see for herself. For nearly a week she hadn't tested the ice. Now she saw that it had moved far beyond the island. She walked out into a biting wind. The snow had melted and frozen by turns, and the ice was uneven, but solid. She threw the stone ahead of her, retrieved it, threw it again. When she looked back she saw the whole island behind her and realized with a thrill of fright that she could go on and on this way straight across the lake.

On the first good day she'd leave, a sunny, windless day with no threat of a sudden change in the weather. It would be foolish to be caught out on the lake in a snow storm.

But days passed and the sky remained cloudy. Snow fell. A week went by, and the weather hadn't improved. She made all her preparations for leaving, waited another few days, and then couldn't wait any longer. Tomorrow, if it wasn't snowing, she'd leave.

The next day she was up at first light. A gray morning, a paper-gray sky. She would go. It might be weeks before the sun shone. At least today it wasn't snowing.

Everything had been done, but she lingered. The coals glowed. They'd still be warm tonight.

The warm rocks, the dimness—how beautiful the cave seemed to her, close and safe, a mantle of warm stone. It was hard to leave.

She wore three shirts, raccoon shawl over her head, the deerskin leggings flapping loosely over her overalls. At the edge of the island, she hesitated. Was she ready? In the knapsack she had her sleeping bag, ax, shovel, the precious remaining matches, and all the dried venison, seeds, and nuts. Crossing the ice should be simple, might only take a few hours, but things could go wrong. There would be places on the ice where she'd be afraid to go. Detours. She might get lost and come to the wrong shore.

She looked out across the ice, that bleak uninviting waste. She would be safe in the cave. With the rest of the venison and fish she could last the winter. Maybe she should wait another day, or wait for the sun. She stepped out on the ice, started out slowly, testing the ice every few steps. Nothing lay before her but fields of snow contoured by the wind, the sun on her right, dim behind the clouds. Whiteness all around. For the last time she looked back at the island. The island, her island. Good-bye . . . good-bye . . .

# Chapter 22

The wind was unrelenting. It bit at her cheeks, dug at her through her clothes. Under the poncho she tucked her hands high in her armpits, trudged on, aware of her breath and the crunch of her snowshoes.

A squall of blowing snow whipped around her, turned her white, and drove sprays of sandlike snow down her neck. The snowshoes made her gait awkward. Step followed step. . . . The monotonous crunch of the snowshoes led her on.

How much longer? *On, on,* the snowshoes said. *Go on.* . . . Where am I? . . . Do you know where we're going? . . . *On, on.* . . . I should have seen land by now. . . . *On, go on.* . . . How long has it been? . . . Am I almost across the ice? . . . *On, on, go on.* . . . *On, on, on* . . .

The tie on the right snowshoe broke loose. She trudged on with one shoe flapping loosely, till it snapped off. She abandoned it, walked with one foot on top of the snow, the other in deep. She looked ahead, straining to see the mainland through the squalls.

The other snowshoe broke. She kicked it away, sank into the snow with both feet. She moved without being conscious of moving. She was laughing at something Jam was doing. Jam was making faces at her from around the door, and Cleo couldn't stop laughing. . . .

Her feet were strange as if she were above the ground, walking on boxes. "It's a warning," she said, and came awake. "Make a fire," she ordered herself. She had to get off the ice. She looked up at the dim brightness behind the clouds. Behind her she saw the tracks wavering one way and then the other. How long had she been moving without knowing which way she was going? Was she going in circles? She was on a white plain, with a white sky overhead, a wall of white in every direction. . . .

The wind died down. In the distance, just above the white, she saw the mainland, white streaked with black. Still far off. She trudged on. Her feet weren't part of her. She stumbled, fell in the snow, got up, went on. Ran. . . . A forest of trees came down to the edge of the ice. She ran, fell, climbed up on the land.

In a sheltered spot she cleared the snow and built a fire, then removed her boots and held her feet close to the fire. When they were warm again, she rewrapped them in dry rags and pulled on her boots.

Which way now? Which way to Dundee? She hardly hesitated, but turned west along the shore. She followed the shore line, crossing the bays on the ice. As she crossed the land jutting out from a long bay, she suddenly came into sight of Dundee, sitting broad and still above the lake. Its windows were shuttered, no smoke in any of its four chimneys. It appeared enormous, austere, and unreal.

Almost seven months before, she'd set out from this place. Was anybody here? The paths were snowed over. Everywhere, the smooth white glaze of untouched snow. Frank's cabin was on the other side of the main house, close to the gates. She pushed through the deep snow. Everything would be all right once she found Frank.

Dogs came running at her, a black Labrador and a growling German shepherd.

"Fritz! Blackie! Over here!" The dogs ran to meet a man striding toward her. She saw the heavy mackinaw, the orange hunting cap. Frank.

He seemed huge. He had a revolver in his hand. "Don't you read signs? No trespassing."

Cleo nodded, so tired she couldn't speak.

The gun moved from one hand to the other. "What's the matter with you? Are you in trouble? Who are you?"

"Cleo," she said.

"What?" He leaned toward her.

"Cleo," she said once more. "Cleo, *Cleo*."

He looked at her closely. "Cleo . . . is that what you're saying? Cleo Murphy?"

She nodded.

"You know where she is?"

Cleo pointed to herself.

He put the revolver in his mackinaw pocket. "Come inside and warm up. I'll give you a cup of coffee. I want to talk to you."

The sudden heat inside the cabin made her queasy. It was stifling, and there was a thick greasy smell. She ran back to the door, afraid she'd throw up.

"Where are you going?"

The spasm passed. She sank down against the wall, and pulled off her boots. The electric light was in her eyes. She turned her face to the wall, and threw off her fur shawl. Her feet, her face, her whole body was burning. She threw off everything, leaving only her torn jeans and shirt.

Frank brought her a green mug of coffee with milk and sugar. "Drink this." He pulled up a chair. "You don't have to sit on the floor. Here, sit up here." He smelled of tobacco. "I want to talk to you."

She remained on the floor holding the green mug in her hands.

"What do you know about Cleo Murphy? When did you see her last? Do you understand what I'm saying to you? Who told you about her?"

Cleo sipped the coffee. It was terribly sweet, and she felt it instantly in her stomach, spreading a warm glow through her limbs. "I am Cleo."

He looked puzzled. A big man who didn't change his way of thinking easily.

"I am Cleo Murphy."

He laid his broad hands on his knees. He was annoyed. Wanted this nonsense to stop. "What are you talking about? Do you know who Cleo Murphy is?" He produced a newspaper and showed her a photo on the front page. "Is this the girl you saw?" The folded headline said, "Heiress Missing. Search Continues on West Coast."

"Do you recognize her?"

It was an old school photo of herself, smiling pleasantly at the camera. Was that her, that bland, respectful, round-cheeked face?

Frank sat next to her, holding the newspaper.

"Do you know what I'm saying to you? There's a reward. Money, beaucoup money, if you know where she is."

He was sitting beside her, looking at her, looking at her picture. "Do you have any idea who Cleo Murphy is? Do you know her father?"

Cleo felt weary, leaned back. "I told you. I am Cleo Murphy."

"You are, eh? Then tell me where you've been."

She gestured to the lake.

"Duck Island, you mean?"

She nodded.

"Come on, the truth, you're not fooling me. I'm too old to be fooled. There's nobody on that island. The cabin burned down two years ago. Where'd you live?"

"A cave."

"A cave on Duck Island?"

"Yes."

A look of doubt crossed his face. "I've been to the island. I didn't see you there. If you're Cleo, why didn't you answer me when I called? Nobody's on that island without me knowing it. Now I want the truth. Who are you, and where'd you come from?"

"The island. I crossed the ice." The heat was making her drowsy. She wanted to lie down and sleep, but he kept questioning her. When had she gone to the island? How did she get there? Had she really been there all this time? What did she eat?

"Not much." Cleo stretched out on the floor, the raccoon skin under her cheek.

"What are you doing now? Don't sleep there. There's a couch. You can use the bed. Cleo?"

Behind her shut eyes, she saw her fire smoldering in the rocks, the hot reddish coals . . .

# Chapter 23

"Listen, Mr. Murphy, I didn't believe it myself at first. I've never seen anything like it." Cleo heard the rumble of Frank's deep voice in her ear. To awaken she had to climb up from a great depth. She could see the light above her, but kept slipping back. Her eyes opened, then shut. Wooden roof . . . exposed rafters . . . the smell of coffee, tobacco . . . a blanket over her. She had to remember to thank Frank, not take anything for granted. Nobody had to do things for her.

"No, she hasn't told me very much. Walked in about an hour ago, half frozen, hair all over her face, and she won't get off the floor."

He listened. "Right. I asked her. Said she took it. Well, she knew where the key was, or found it. Yes, she's all right. She seems all right. Can you believe it? Living on Duck Island, in a cave, all this time."

He glanced over at Cleo. "She's awake now. You want to talk to her?" Frank motioned to Cleo. "Mr. Murphy—your father—wants to talk to you."

She leaned against the wall. "Hello?"

"Cleo?"

"Hello, Dad. . . . It's me."

"Cleo?"

"Yes, it's me. Cleo."

There was a moment's silence. "It is you?"

"Yes."

"Are you all right? Are you sick? How do you feel?" He was talking loudly. "Do you need a doctor? I can have a doctor flown—"

"No, I'm all right, Dad, just a little tired—"

"It is you, isn't it? Well! Welcome home. Where have you been?"

"Duck Island."

"All this time?"

"Yes."

"We've been looking for you. Did you know that we thought you were dead? Did you realize we thought you were dead?"

"I'm sorry. . . . I'm really sorry. I would have come sooner, but I couldn't."

"Wait a minute—your grandmother wants to talk to you."

"Cleo, is it you?" Her grandmother's voice was full. "Are you all right, dear? Is it really you?"

"I'm okay, Grandma. I'm fine. I'm sorry I caused you so much trouble."

"I knew you were alive. There were people who thought you might have taken your own life. I never believed it. I told Charles I was only afraid that you'd gotten into the hands of unsavory people . . . you know . . . who would influence you."

"Nobody influenced me, Grandma."

Her grandmother was crying. "We were so worried. . . . You don't know . . ."

Her father came on the phone. "Where were you?" he asked again.

"Duck Island."

"You really were there?"

"Yes. My canoe got smashed in a storm."

"Frank went there. Did you see him? Did you know he was there?"

"Yes, but—" Suddenly she was overcome with a profound sense of unreality—this phone conversation, this room, the wall she leaned against, Frank sitting on the couch, listening. . . . She closed her eyes, almost wishing it would all disappear—that she was back on the island. She felt so tired.

"I can't talk anymore right now, Dad."

"Of course, of course. We'll talk again. We have

a lot to talk about. Get rested, dear. Let me speak to Frank."

She handed Frank the phone. "Your bathroom?" He motioned toward the door near the kitchen.

She stayed in the bathroom a long time. It was a tiny room, purely functional, with a sink, toilet, and shower stall, but everything amazed her. She looked at herself curiously in the mirror, then stood under the shower, turning the water on and off, soaping herself, then showering and resoaping herself. She washed her hair several times, then stood under the warm water. All that heat just by turning a knob.

She slept on the couch that night, and in the morning Frank found her a pair of his nephew's blue jeans and an old blue flannel shirt. She rolled up the sleeves and remained barefoot till it was time to leave.

The arrangement was that Frank would drive her to Toronto, where they would catch a plane for Chicago.

"You don't have to take me all that way."

"You don't think I'm letting you out of my sight now? How about breakfast?"

"You've done so much for me already. . . . I want to thank you. I really appreciate everything, but you don't have to bother about breakfast." She got up. "Just tell me—"

"Sit down," he told her. He brought out milk, bread, eggs. "When you live alone you get used to your own way of doing things."

Yes, she understood that. It made her feel strange now—not doing for herself.

She tasted everything, but ate little. "I'm not very hungry," she said.

"You're right to be careful. Takes a while to get back to normal food."

All the way to Toronto in Frank's truck she thought about meeting her father and grand-mother. She and Frank talked a little, but in the airplane she slept, dreaming that she was back on the island.

Her grandmother and father were waiting when she and Frank got off the plane at O'Hare Airport. She saw her father first, head above the waiting crowd. He kissed her, something he never did, and she kissed him back, then kissed her grandmother, tasted face powder, that faint repugnant smell, and felt an unexpected rush of emotion. This was her family, all she had left in the world.

Her father took her knapsack then turned to Frank, who was taking the next plane back to Toronto. Cleo thanked him again for everything he'd done for her.

"You're so thin," her grandmother said. "I can't get used to it."

As they made their way down the long tunnel-like corridors her father and grandmother guided her through the sea of hurrying people. She felt again, as she'd felt ever since she'd come to Dundee, that she was being carried along, not exactly against her will, but somehow out of touch with herself.

In the car, in that plush, still interior, she felt the gritty energy of the city flailing her, coming at her from every angle. Traffic lights, signs, buildings flashing past—the whole crazy energy of the city coming at her.

Her grandmother kept glancing at her, at the raccoon fur in her lap. "What is that animal thing?" Her grandmother's pale, well-tended hands hovered over the fur. "Did you buy it?"

Cleo ran her fingers through the raccoon fur, looked at her own brown hands, the broken nails, the white scars where she'd cut herself skinning animals.

"I killed it."

"You killed it!" Her grandmother glanced at Cleo's father.

"What does that mean?" her father said.

Cleo touched the fur. "I killed the deer, too."

"What for?"

"Food."

"You ate it?" her father said.

"Yes."

"I can't believe it. I can't believe this, Charles. Did you have to kill the deer?" her grandmother said to her.

"How did you kill it?" her father asked.

"With a knife."

"A deer is a big animal."

"Not this one. It was lame—and I made a trap."

"And you ate it?"

"Yes. Everything. I cooked the bones."

After that, little more was said on the way home.

Those first days at home were painful. She had changed, and so she thought everything would be different. But at times she felt as if she'd never been away and nothing had changed.

She found the house too hot, the food too rich, and there was too much of it. At meals she ate sparingly, taking little bites, chewing long and carefully. She was quick to rise, to help Mrs. Terrero clear, but too much was made of it.

There were questions. They wanted to know why she'd run away.

*Why?* They kept going back to it.

She tried to tell them about the misery she'd felt after Jam died, how lost she had been.

"It was a shock," her grandmother said. "A terrible shock. I haven't gotten over it yet." She wiped her eyes. "You should have come to us."

"I couldn't, I just couldn't. It wouldn't have helped. Do you understand?" Cleo leaned forward. "Do you understand what I'm saying? Jam was—everything—to me."

"I understand that," her father said. "But why did you go to Duck Island? It seems such a purposeless thing to do. I'm curious—did you have some kind of spiritual experience there? A revelation? I've heard of people who have gone into the wilderness." He smiled, then sipped his coffee. "Indian medicine men, gurus, mystics, who have those moments when they supposedly see everything in a flash of light." Her father's smile—that remote, slightly ironic tone that kept her off—would she ever unravel it?

She had been about to say something about that time she had felt herself rising, that sense of extraordinary happiness. Instead she said, "It was peaceful on the island. I felt good. It was good to do things myself, with my own hands. It gave me a good feeling. I felt I really belonged there."

"You belong here," her grandmother said. "I hope you don't feel out of place at home with your own family."

"An outdoor girl," her father said. "I'd never

have thought it. You're an extremist. Did you have to stay away so long? What did you prove?"

"I couldn't leave the island after the storm. The canoe was smashed. I told you. I tried to swim back."

"Swim from Duck Island. That sounds stupid."

"It was."

Her grandmother put her hand over Cleo's. "I don't think I want to hear it again."

Her father suddenly pushed aside his plate.

"Your little escapade kept me very busy."

"What?"

"I was convinced at first that you were kidnapped. That seemed plausible, but then we didn't hear anything from the kidnappers. Except for that curious call to White Mountain Camp that your grandmother never made."

"Dad—"

"We thought it was the kidnappers giving themselves more time. But it was you, wasn't it? You were the one who wanted more time."

"Yes—"

"Well, you fooled your father. The detectives I hired and the police said you were probably a runaway. I insisted you weren't the type. One daughter buried, one running away. I can only think you were influenced. Who was it?"

"Who?" she said. "Nobody."

"There was somebody with you. I believe there must have been."

"No. I was alone."

"Did it all yourself? Marvelous." His disbelief, sarcasm, and anger made her wince.

"Do you know how long it was?"

"Seven months."

"A long time between phone calls."

"I'm sorry."

"I'm sure you are! I had a report about a girl who answered your description who'd been stopped at the Mexican border with drugs."

"I've never used drugs."

"Well, how the hell would I know? You didn't leave any directives. I sent my man flying down there for nothing. And that wasn't the only place."

Cleo pushed back her chair. What a mess it was. "I'm sorry I caused you pain." What else could she say? There had been reasons for what she'd done. "I didn't expect you to like it, Dad. I didn't go away to annoy you, or upset you and Grandma. What I did—well—I have no excuse."

"Is that all?" Her grandmother said. "We haven't said anything up to now. We wanted to give you time to adjust, to think things over. You say you're sorry, but I don't see any real remorse. Do you know what those seven months were like for us? The waiting, the not knowing, the worry."

Her grandmother pressed her hand over her lips.

"I'm sorry, Grandmother," Cleo said again. "I said I was sorry. I mean it. I never wanted to hurt you or Dad. But I had to go. I'm not sorry about that."

After that, they were wary with her. She felt that they looked at her as if she were peculiar, odd, perhaps worse. Her grandmother wanted her to see a psychiatrist. Cleo refused. She had nothing to talk to a psychiatrist about.

"Are you ready to go back to St. Ives?" her grandmother said one day.

"I don't know if I want to return there."

"You don't? Then where do you think you want to go?"

"I don't know. Nowhere right now."

She walked a lot. After she was inside a while she had to get out, where she could see the sky and trees, or go down by the lake and look out over the sea that was Lake Michigan.

She felt she should go away, perhaps return to school, but for a time she couldn't make up her mind.

She missed seeing animals. At a shopping mall she spent a long time in a pet shop. The birds interested her, the parakeets, canaries, parrots. One large green parrot especially reminded her of Owl. When she put her hand into the cage, the bird's claw closed around her finger. "I used to have an owl," she said to the tall boy at the counter.

"What kind of owl was it?" he asked.

"A screech owl, maybe. Crows had attacked him and he couldn't fly."

They talked for a while and when Cleo left, he went to the door with her. "My name's Dan." When she was down the arcade and glanced back, he was still looking after her.

She spent time in the library looking at books about the wilderness and threatened animals. She thought about being a naturalist, somebody who studied animals, was outdoors a lot. It was possible. She didn't know enough, though, not yet.

"I'm going back to St. Ives," she said to her grandmother one morning over breakfast. She had made up her mind the night before. There was a progression to things. She'd learned it on the island. One step, and then the next, and then the one after that. A progression to the day and to the season and to all of life. School was part of the progression for her.

"St. Ives?" her grandmother said. "I never expected it. I thought we were in for a long siege of indecision, and wandering, and nothing getting done."

"Is that the way you think about me?"

"I don't know how to think about you, Cleo. You are a mystery to me. You have done things that I have never done, never will do, would never want to do. I don't understand why you did them. Some of the things you did are extraordinary. I really marvel at you. I only hope you've returned to normal and are ready to live a normal life again."

"I might be." Cleo squeezed her grandmother's hand. "If we could ever agree on what normal is."

A week later Cleo was on a plane again, this time bound for school. The seat beside her was empty. She sat, stroking the raccoon skin on her lap.

She hadn't forgotten the way she'd been at St. Ives before, in a dream most of the time, only coming alive on vacations when she was with Jam. She didn't want to go back to being like that. She didn't have to. Things had happened—the island had happened. The island . . . the island . . .

She remembered the first time she saw the deer in the inlet and discovered the stream and how the island opened before her. All that movement around her, the swimming creatures, the air vibrating with the hum of insects and birds, the life on the hills and in the water. It was still there, under the snow. She would go back. She closed her eyes, invoked the strength of the island, drew it close around herself.

## About the Author

HARRY MAZER was born in New York. He received the bachelor's degree from Union College, Schenectady, and the master's in education from Syracuse University. His most recent novel, *The Last Mission,* was named an ALA Best Book for Young Adults, as were his earlier books, *The War on Villa Street* and *The Solid Gold Kid* (which was co-authored by his wife, Norma Fox Mazer). All are available in Dell Laurel-Leaf editions. The Mazers live in Jamesville, New York, near Syracuse.